Chris Morphew was born in Sydney in 1985. He spent his childhood drawing comic books and writing stories about dinosaurs and time machines. After school, Chris did a short stint as a primary school teacher – which he thinks is the second-best job in the world – and then started writing for kids and young adults. He lives in Australia.

Follow Chris on Twitter @ChrisMorphew

"THE PHOENIX FILES absolutely blew me away"
Michael Grant, author of *GONE*

UNDERGROUND

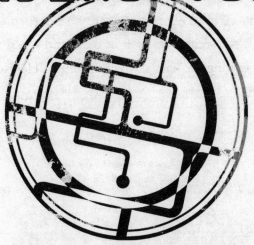

Chris Morphew

THE PHOENIX FILES

SCHOLASTIC

First published in the UK in 2012 by Scholastic Children's Books
An imprint of Scholastic Ltd
Euston House, 24 Eversholt Street
London, NW1 1DB, UK
Registered office: Westfield Road, Southam, Warwickshire, CV47 0RA
SCHOLASTIC and associated logos are trademarks
and/or registered trademarks of Scholastic Inc.

Text © Chris Morphew, 2011
First published in Australia by Hardie Grant Egmont, 2011.
The right of Chris Morphew to be identified as
the author of this work has been asserted by him.

ISBN 978 1407 13119 1

Printed by CPI Group (UK) Ltd, Croydon, CR0 4YY
Papers used by Scholastic Children's Books are made
from wood grown in sustainable forests.

1 3 5 7 9 10 8 6 4 2

www.scholastic.co.uk/zone

To Phil and Meredith Doiner-Harding,
Happy Wedding!

Chapter 1

"Luke Hunter," said the woman, horribly calm, arms folded across a dirty lab coat. "At last. You have no idea how long we've waited for you to arrive."

I looked up, hardly seeing her, eyes watering from the agony in my legs and the fluorescent lights beating down from the ceiling.

I pushed up from the floor, shaking, staring past her into the underground lair or whatever it was that we'd just crashed into. Sinks. Benches. Surgical equipment. Peter strapped to a rusting bed. Jordan clawing towards him.

Pain surged again from the suppressor in my back,

1

dropping my legs out from under me. I cried out, face smashing into the lino, reigniting the nosebleed that Tank had given me back at the crater.

The woman in the lab coat glanced over her glasses at me, indifferent. She turned to her offsider, the spiky-haired maybe-20-year-old Eurasian guy who was apparently her son. "Him first," she said, nudging me with her foot. "Quickly."

She had one of those weirdly proper voices that sounded British but wasn't, like she'd be more at home at a country club than an underground death chamber.

Spiky-Haired Guy nodded and crouched down, grabbing me by the ankles. I tried to kick free, but—

Nothing. No response.

No! I pleaded silently, panic ratcheting up again even through all the pain. *No, please…* I kicked harder – or tried to, anyway – but Shackleton's suppressor had done its job. My legs were no longer taking orders from my brain.

But I could still *feel* everything.

The woman bent down, clasping cold hands around my wrists.

"Hey! *Let go of him!*" shouted Jordan from across the room, dragging herself up against the foot of

Peter's bed with her one good arm. Still fighting.

The woman ignored her, locking eyes with Spiky-Haired Guy. "Ready? One, two, *three*."

I screamed, fire coursing through my legs as they hauled me up off the ground.

"Jordan, get out! Now!" Peter begged. Like I was irrelevant, except as a distraction.

He was drowned out by Jordan's tortured groan as she slumped back to the floor, levelled by her own suppressor. She lay there gasping, face hidden in a mess of braids.

There was another bed across the room. The two lab coats lugged me toward it, sidestepping around Jordan's shaking body. The ground blurred under me. I coughed, spraying blood.

We were dead.

We might've escaped Calvin by coming down here, but it seemed like all we'd done was swap one set of psychopaths for another.

Pain surged through me again as they hoisted me up on to the bed. "Please..." I murmured in the moment before they dropped me. "Why are you—?"

I hit the mattress and a mouthful of lumpy pillow muffled the rest of my question. A hand pressed me into the bed and I heard a sound like a zipper as one of them pulled a strap down tight across the top of my legs. Two more straps came down over my ankles.

I twisted around, smearing blood across the pillow. Jordan was still on the floor, on her side now, hand out behind her, clawing through her backpack.

Spiky-Haired Guy turned to look at her.

"STOP!" I shouted with all the energy I had left, dragging his attention back to me. "Let me go! Let – ARGH!"

Another wave of pain from the suppressor, even worse because I couldn't move properly. I gritted my teeth, writhing under the restraints.

"Hold him still," the woman ordered, and I felt Spiky-Haired Guy's weight come down on my back, pinning my arms to my sides. Another strap tightened across my shoulders.

I turned my head just in time to see a huge needle sweep across my field of vision.

"No-no-no!" I said. *"Wait!"*

And then she was plunging it into me, digging into the small of my back, magnifying the pain all over again. I bit down on the pillow, screaming into it, almost throwing up, and then—

A slow, creeping numbness. Starting at the needle-point and spreading out across my skin.

4

At first, my body couldn't even process what was happening. The pain had been so intense, so complete, that I'd almost forgotten what it was like to feel anything else. But then the numbness reached my legs, trickling downwards, melting the pain away. And for a minute, I stopped fighting and just collapsed into the bed, heart machine-gunning in my chest.

The woman pulled the needle out and Spiky-Haired Guy got off me. The anaesthetic kept creeping, rolling down to the ends of my toes. Panic rose in my throat. Because now my legs were *gone*.

No feeling. No movement.

There was another groan from the floor. Jordan had shifted out of view, somewhere near the foot of my bed. Peter was straining against his straps, staring down at her.

Then a clatter of metal and the woman stepped back into my line of sight, armed with a glinting scalpel.

"No!" I said, struggling against the straps across my body. "Please – you don't—"

"Soren," snapped the woman, and a second later her son was pinning me to the bed again.

He smacked me in the head, clumsy and awkward, like a kid. "Shut your mouth— *Nngh!*"

He jumped off me, swearing viciously.

I caught a glimpse of Jordan rolling away from him, a biro clutched in her left hand.

"For goodness" sake," the woman muttered. "Deal with her, would you?"

"NO!" roared Peter from across the room. *"Don't touch her!"*

Spiky-Haired Guy bent down to grab Jordan, then hesitated as a weird noise started buzzing out from the fluorescent tubes in the ceiling.

The split second was all Jordan needed. With a grunt, she swung herself toward him, smashing a fist into Spiky-Haired Guy's face. He drew back, and Jordan fell to the ground again, wincing at the still-bleeding gash Tank had left in her shoulder half an hour ago.

The woman strode over to help her son, pulling the cap off a metal tube that reminded me of the auto-injector pens my dad carried around for his anaphylaxis.

"GET AWAY!" Peter's whole bed rattled violently as he raged against his restraints. "GET AWAY FROM HER!"

The lights buzzed again, and for a second they dimmed away altogether, throwing us into darkness.

"I thought you fixed the generator," said the woman.

"I *did*," said Spiky-Haired Guy as the lights brightened again.

He grabbed Jordan's forearms and pinned her on her back. Then he paused, staring down at her, like his brain had short-circuited or something. His thumbs brushed over her skin and I felt a whole different kind of sick.

Jordan jerked up and spat in his face.

"Foolish girl," the woman snapped, crouching next to her. "Do you think I don't know what they've put in you?"

"LET HER GO!" Peter screamed, red-faced.

The lights buzzed louder, flickering on and off.

Jordan flailed around madly, but there was no movement below her waist. The woman took aim at Jordan's thigh with the pen thing.

"Wait!" I shouted. "Please, just *wait* a minute!"

Peter roared again, not even words this time.

SMASH!

The lights exploded above our heads, plunging us into complete darkness. Shards of glass rained down on top of me.

"What was that?" Spiky-Haired Guy shrieked.

I heard a shuffling sound, like someone feeling their way across the floor, then Jordan cried out again.

More rattling from Peter's bed.

"Jordan!" I yelled.

A muffled groan, then nothing.

"Sedate the others!" barked the woman's voice. *"Now!"*

Footsteps darted across the room. There was a clattering sound – one of them running into something – then a tiny *click*. A torch beam flashed to life from somewhere behind me.

The beam swept over my body and I flinched, like it was going to cut me open.

Craning my neck, I saw Spiky-Haired Guy fumbling in the torchlight, ripping the cap off another metal pen.

I felt nothing as he jammed it into my thigh, but a sudden heaviness spread through me – through every part of me that could still feel, anyway – weighing me down into the bed. I squeezed my eyes shut, trying to shake it off.

My head slumped back down against the pillow.

And then—

Chapter 2

I woke up slowly, head pounding, nauseated.

I tried to stretch out my arms. They were still tied down, but—

Hang on.

The lights were back on again. I was sitting up, plastic cable ties pinning my ankles and wrists to a rickety metal chair.

Out of the laboratory. Alone in an empty room.

Although "room" was being kind of generous. This place looked more like a cave than anything that had been built on purpose. Only one of the four walls was even vertical. The other three were big, rippling

9

messes of concrete with bits of wood and metal jutting out all over the place – like the room had started melting and then turned solid again.

There was a narrow, rusting door opposite me, in the one wall that was still intact. The door had a window in it – at least, I assumed there used to be glass there – which looked out on another room that seemed to be in no better shape than this one.

It was as though someone had tried to bury this whole place in concrete but done a really dodgy job of it. Or maybe changed their minds and tried to dig it out again.

"Jordan!" I yelled. "JORDAN!"

No response.

"PETER!" I tried.

Nothing.

My brain was powering up again. Just enough to let the panic back in. I pushed myself up as much as I could, straining against the cable ties. The old chair creaked under me but refused to give way. I heaved forward, wincing as the ties dug in to my arms and my—

My legs.

I could feel them again. I could *move* them again.

I dropped back into the seat, mind tracing back

through the chaos in the laboratory.

The woman, stooping to stab Jordan full of sedative.

Foolish girl. Do you think I don't know what they've put in you?

And then it clicked. That was why the Co-operative hadn't been able to track Peter down here.

These people, whoever they were, had found a way to remove his suppressor. Or keep them from tracing it, at least. And now they'd done the same to mine.

But given that I was trapped underground and tied to a chair, I was guessing they weren't too concerned with looking out for *us*. They just didn't want the Co-operative to find *them*.

I went back to fighting the cable ties, twisting my arms against them, trying to snap them off, but all I managed to do was scrape a few layers of skin off my wrists.

I stopped to get my breath back, eyes down at my shoes. My ankles were strapped tight to the legs of the chair, but my feet were almost flat on the ground. If I could get up on my toes, I might be able to get across to one of those bits of shrapnel sticking out of the wall...

I craned my neck, looking for something close.

A little way off to my left, I spotted the twisted remains of an old metal sign. Most of it was buried in the concrete, but in the corner I could make out what looked like a company logo: the words VATTEL COMPLEX, stamped next to an all-too-familiar black spiral shape. It was the same spiral that Mike, Cathryn and Tank had tattooed on their arms. The word *Vattel* seemed weirdly familiar too, but I couldn't put my finger on why.

Forget it, I told myself. Right now, all that mattered was that the corner of that sign looked sharp enough to cut me free. If I could get to it. Probably sharp enough to slice my arm open too, if I didn't aim it right.

I settled back into the chair, psyching myself up. I rocked slowly back and forth, knowing I only had one chance to get on my feet. Push too far forward and I'd go right over with no way to break my fall.

You can do it, I told myself. *You can do it.*

Actually, you know what? Maybe you can't.

But you have no other plan, so get on with it.

I took a breath, clutching the arms of the chair, and threw myself forward.

The two back legs lifted off the ground. I rolled on to the balls of my feet. Staggered, finding my balance— Then lost it again and lurched forward, toppling in slow motion, slamming my knees against the concrete floor. The ground smashed into my nose as the chair fell, dragging me down on to my side. I lay there, tears streaming.

And it was only then that I saw the ancient-looking security camera gazing down at me from the corner of the ceiling.

I don't know how long I was lying there like that.

But it was long enough for the blood to clot up and block my nose. Long enough for me to realize there was no way I was ever getting up without help. Long enough to think that pneumonia was a definite possibility if I spent much longer on this freezing concrete.

Eventually, though, I heard footsteps in the room outside. Then the door clunked open.

It was Spiky-Haired Guy, out of his lab coat now, dragging another chair in behind him.

He crouched behind me and I flinched.

"Calm down," he said, hauling my chair upright. I grunted as the cable ties tore at my skin, and again as the four legs thudded back to the concrete.

Spiky-Haired Guy brought his chair over and sat down opposite me. He was dressed in a hoodie and jeans that were too new to have come from down here. Mike and his friends must have stolen them for him. Handy to have a few secret slaves to go shopping for you.

He leant forward, closer than necessary. Close enough for me to feel his breath on my face. For the first time, I noticed how unnaturally pale his skin was.

Guess they don't get a whole lot of sun down here.

I waited for him to back off, but he just hovered there in front of me, examining me, like I was some fascinating exhibit in a museum.

My fingers tightened around the arms of my chair. "Why are you doing this to us?"

He jumped back, like he'd forgotten I could talk, then quickly recovered himself. "You know why."

Which was so ridiculously far from true that my brain couldn't even generate a response.

"I'm Soren," he said, stretching out a hand. It hung there for a second as he stared down at my bound arms. Then he shoved it back into the pocket of his hoodie and sat back, waiting for me to respond. Like he didn't already know exactly who I was.

His eyes twitched, flashing up at the camera. There was something weird about the way he moved. It was all quick, jerking motions. Like a caged animal.

Which, if he really had been down here since before Phoenix was built, might not be too far from the truth.

He gave me a few more seconds, then spoke again. "All right, Luke—"

"Can I have some water?" I asked, suddenly aware of how dry my throat was.

"No," said Soren automatically. But then his eyes flickered again, like he wasn't sure that was the right answer. "OK. OK, yes. But one glass. That's all." He got up and left the room, pulling the door shut.

I closed my eyes, trying to get my head together. *He's just a person,* I thought.

These were the "overseers" that Mike, Cathryn and Tank had been following all this time? The way they'd been talking, it was like they thought there was something – I don't know – *supernatural* about them.

I waited, listening for Soren's return. But then I heard something else.

A muffled voice, coming from somewhere nearby.

"JORDAN!" I shouted. "JOR—!"

"Hey, *shut up!*" snapped Soren, reappearing behind the smashed window. He pushed the door open and returned to his seat, clutching a very murky glass of water.

I leant forward and he held the glass to my lips, tipping it toward me. It was gritty and tasted like metal, and he poured it down my throat way too fast. I coughed half of it back up again, splashing water down the front of my shirt.

"OK," said Soren, putting the empty glass down on the floor. "OK, now you're going to talk. I would like to know *exactly* what his plan is."

His voice had the same too-proper edge as his mother's. But there was something else too. A kind of stiltedness, as though he'd learnt all the theory about how this "conversation" stuff was supposed to work, but hadn't actually tried it out until now. Which, again, possibly wasn't all that much of a stretch.

Soren folded his arms.

I looked back at him, head still throbbing like something was about to burst out of it. "Whose plan? Shackleton's?"

Soren's right hand blurred out and smacked me in the side of the head.

"*Peter's* plan," he spat, looking like two people for a second as my eyes struggled back into focus. "This weapon of yours. You're going to tell me where he's keeping it, and why you and your girlfriend—"

"What? No, Tabitha is *Shackleton's* weapon! And

we're trying to stop him, not— Hey, no-no-no, wait!" I shrank back as Soren brought his hand around again. "Just *wait*, OK? Listen to me."

Soren paused mid-swing, considering. He lowered his arm.

"Look," I said, still bracing myself, "I know Cathryn told you guys that we were behind all this, but she's *wrong*, OK? That DVD she saw us watching – it was a test video that Shackleton—"

"Do you really believe that's why we brought you here?" said Soren. "Do you think we've only just now worked you three out?"

I shivered, the water he'd spilled down my front freezing cold against my skin.

No, I realized. No, this went back way further than that.

On our way into this place, Jordan and I had stumbled on to a scene straight out of a serial killer movie: a whole wall crammed full of photos and articles and print-outs and maps, dating back almost two decades. All of it somehow connected to Jordan, Peter and me – a giant timeline of our lives.

Long before we knew Phoenix existed, before the town had even been built, Soren and his mum had been watching us.

"He will turn on you," Soren breathed, leaning forward again. "He does not deserve your loyalty."

I turned my head, twisting away from him.

Soren grabbed the front of my shirt with both hands. "Tell me about Tobias."

Who?

"I thought we were talking about Peter," I said.

Soren threw me against the chair, almost knocking me to the floor again. "WHERE IS HE?"

"I don't know!" I said. "I don't know, OK? I don't even know who Tobias *is.*"

Soren swung his arm wide, cracking me across the face with the back of his hand.

"Stop!" I shouted. "Where is this coming from? Who told you we were—?"

I broke off. Soren's expression had shifted. He was looking at me like I'd just told him something important.

"You really don't know what he's capable of, do you?" he murmured, only just loud enough for me to hear, and went back to staring at me like I was an inanimate object.

I shifted in my seat. My left leg was cramping up, but I could barely move it without the cable tie ripping further into my ankle.

My eyes drifted to the sign on the wall, and a memory surfaced in my brain. An article Jordan had read out from that fake *Time* magazine, about the original owner of the land Phoenix was built on.

"Remi Vattel!" I said. "The woman out there – your mum – is she—?"

"How do you know that name?" Soren demanded.

"It was – we read about her in—" I hesitated.

Soren looked ready to take another swing. "Remi Vattel is dead," he said.

And suddenly he was leaving. He grabbed the back of his chair and dragged it toward the door.

"Wait!" I said. "Jordan and Peter – what have you done with them?"

"They are fine," said Soren.

"But—"

"*We're* not murderers, Luke." He walked out, switch-ing the lights off behind him.

Friday 26 June
48 days

For a while – hours, maybe – I sat there in the dark-ness, jumping at every creaking pipe and distant, echoing footstep. But I must have fallen asleep at some point, because I didn't see the light flashing around in the next room until it was right at my door.

There was a shuffling noise outside, and then a torch came glaring in through the window frame, catching me in the face. I groaned, squinting away from the sudden brightness.

The light disappeared for a second, and I heard the door swing open. A figure dashed toward me, almost invisible. The torch swept the room and I caught a glimpse of her face.

"Jordan!"

"Hey," she whispered, crouching down next to my chair. "You ready to get out of here or what?"

Chapter 3

**Friday 26 June
48 days**

"Are you all right?" I asked, trying to get a proper look at her. The torch flashed past her arm and I saw red rings around her wrist. "How did you get away?"

"With this," she said, holding up a tiny blade and getting to work on one of the cable ties. "From my pocket knife. I snapped it off and hid it when the lights went out."

"Hid it where?" I asked, lifting my arm as the first tie snapped free.

"Under here," said Jordan. She shone the torch up to her hair and held out a braid.

I stared at her. "You're incredible. You know that, right?"

"You're welcome," she said, cutting a second tie and moving down to my ankles.

"Where's Peter?"

"Don't know. Back at that lab place, maybe? It seemed like that was where they were keeping him."

"Yeah," I said, feeling my right foot spring free. "Wherever that is."

I brought my hands up to my face, testing it with my fingertips. Everything was swollen and stinging.

Jordan cut the last cable tie. She pocketed the blade and pulled me to my feet. "C'mon."

"Wait," I said, feeling the ache in my legs. "What's our plan here?"

"Find Peter and get out," said Jordan impatiently.

"Then what? We can't go home. Not after yesterday."

"We have to!" said Jordan. "We've been gone too long already. If my parents freak out about this…"

"Yeah, but what about Calvin?" I said. Getting gunned down by the Chief of Security wasn't exactly a solution.

"What about *them?*" said Jordan, throwing a hand out toward the doorway. "That Kara woman – she's—"

"Kara?" I said. "The mum?"

"Yeah. She didn't come to you?"

I shook my head. "I got the guy. Soren."

"Well, trust me," said Jordan. "We don't want to mess with this woman."

We don't want to mess with Calvin either, I thought.

But then Jordan pulled me toward the door again and, as usual, I shoved my survival instinct aside and limped after her.

"Besides," said Jordan, "at least now we don't have the suppressors to worry about."

I brushed a hand down over the small of my back and felt a neat row of stitches, confirming my suspicion from before. I was free. Finally free of it.

About time *something* went right for us.

We stepped out into the room I'd seen through the little window. Another half-destroyed cave-like place, twice as big as the one we'd just left. A worn-out leather couch sat against the wall opposite us. Next to it, a couple of safety helmets hung from a rusty pipe stabbing out from the concrete.

A hallway stretched out on either side of us. Nothing but darkness in both directions.

"This way," whispered Jordan, shifting off to our right.

"How do you know?"

"I don't. But I came from the other way and it's even more destroyed back there."

We kept moving, Jordan shining the torch in front of us, lighting up more of the same misshapen concrete and debris. In a few places, a metal beam or a bit of pipe stretched clear across the corridor, lodged into the walls on both sides.

There were gaps in the walls too, with more rooms behind them, but most of the doors were half-buried in concrete. It was hard to tell whether this was an actual hallway we were walking down, or just a tunnel that had been cleared through all the rubble.

"Have you ever seen *The Wizard of Oz?*" Jordan whispered.

"Huh?" I said, almost tripping on a lump of concrete bulging up from the floor. "What, you think we should try clicking our heels together?"

"Georgia's obsessed with it," said Jordan. "There's this one scene that cracks her up every time. You know at the end, where Toto pulls back the curtain and they find out that the "Great and Powerful Oz" is really just some old guy pulling a bunch of levers? Georgia thinks it's the funniest thing in the world."

"Uh-huh," I said. She probably had a point, but I was too busy watching the path ahead to get what it was.

Jordan gave me a look, like I was being difficult. "Somehow I don't think this is quite what Mike and the others have in mind when they picture their "overseers"."

She froze. There was light up ahead. A dim, flickering glow, shining out from behind a door to our right. One of the few that still looked openable. Jordan switched off her torch and crept forward.

As we got closer, I could hear noises coming from inside the room. Bubbling water and a low, steady humming sound. Why were they so familiar?

Jordan paused at the door, listening. Then she reached out and pushed it open. I tensed, ready to run.

"Huh," said Jordan. "Anyone hungry?"

It was a pantry. At least, it was now. The room looked like it used to be another lab or something, but now all the shelves and benches were piled up with food. Mike and his friends had definitely been keeping busy.

Off to the side was the source of the light and the noise: rows of vegetables, suspended in plastic troughs filled with cloudy white liquid. Harsh lights beat down on them from above.

A hydroponics bay. Like a scaled-down version of

the massive one that secretly provided Phoenix with all its fresh food.

"This room isn't as messed up as the others," Jordan said, moving through the shadows. "Whatever happened to this place, I think it happened back the way we came."

"We should keep going," I said.

"Hang on." She scanned the wall ahead of her, then pulled a chocolate bar from one of the shelves. "You want one?"

"Are you serious? Jordan, we need to—" I stopped in the doorway, watching her rip off the wrapper. Realising how hungry I was. "Actually – yes."

Jordan chucked over a Mars bar, stuffed a couple more into her back pocket, and followed me out the door. She flicked the torch back on and we continued up the hallway, wolfing down the chocolate as we went.

After a few metres, the concrete tunnel straightened out into a proper hallway. The walls were still cracked and crumbling, but they were properly vertical now, and there was no more random junk poking out of them.

It looked like Jordan was right. The further we walked, the more intact everything seemed to be, which hopefully meant we were getting closer to the place where we'd come in.

"Do you think it's just them down here?" I whispered through a mouthful of chocolate. "Just the two of them?"

She shrugged. "I think there *used* to be more. I mean, all these labs and stuff— It must have been, like, a research centre or something, right?"

"I guess so," I said. "So where did everybody go?"

Jordan shone the torch around, as though she was expecting the answer to be written up on the wall somewhere. She turned to say something but then, suddenly, we were at the end of the hallway. There was another door in front of us, already open, leading into a little room with a row of sleeping computers along the wall. I tapped one of the keyboards and the screen flashed on. Camera footage of the place I'd just escaped from. The rest of the room was piled high with boxes, all taped up and numbered. And off to the left, through another open door—

"Peter!" Jordan hissed.

Right where we'd left him, still stuck to the bed, still unconscious. Extra straps buckled over his arms and forehead.

We raced inside. There was a light stretching over

the bed. I switched it on.

"Peter!" said Jordan again, shaking him. "Peter, time to go!"

"Wha— ?" he murmured. "No, don't – don't—" His eyes sprung open. "*Jordan!*"

"Shh!" she warned.

"Sorry." Peter blinked hard. "The entrance— There's a panel on the wall in the next room. I don't know what you press to get out, but—"

"Right," said Jordan, already on her way.

"Check the cameras first!" I said, undoing the strap across Peter's forehead. "Make sure security isn't still up there."

She ran back into the next room, where Kara and Soren had hooked into the Co-operative's security feeds.

"Thanks," said Peter, twisting around to watch Jordan as I freed his head.

"No worries."

"I mean, I realize we're probably all still dead, but…"

"Yeah." I pulled back the strap from his chest. "Things haven't exactly improved while you've been down here."

"Calvin just walked into the security centre," said

Jordan, poking her head through the door. "No guards at the entrance either. I think we're OK." She disappeared again.

"Get my hands," said Peter urgently.

"Right." I pried the strap off his right arm, then moved down to free his legs, leaving Peter to take care of the other arm himself. I leant across to look through the door, trying to see where Jordan—

A harsh, electronic blare came rushing in from the hallway. An alarm.

Guess that means Jordan got the entrance open.

"Hey!" said Peter urgently. "C'mon!"

I got back to work. Peter's other arm was loose by now. He sat up and we got stuck into the last two buckles on his legs.

More noise. Voices and running feet.

"Ah, crap," Peter muttered, glancing across at an unopened door behind us. One more pull and his left leg was undone.

Jordan came tearing into the room. "Need help?"

"No. Go!" I said. "Got it covered!"

"But—"

"GO!" Peter shouted.

She turned back and sprinted for the stairs.

I saw Peter struggling with the last strap and

reached out to help him. "No, I got it," he said, shoving me away. He gave the buckle another jerk, and it finally came loose enough for him to—

Bang!

The door behind us flew open and Kara and Soren came rushing into the room, barefoot, dressed in matching pyjamas.

"Stop!" Kara boomed.

"No thanks," said Peter, shuffling across the bed.

Soren leapt at me.

I ducked under his arms and ran for the surveillance room. Glancing back, I saw Kara reeling away as Peter threw a punch at her. He twisted around and sprung away from the bed.

I realized our mistake a second before he did.

There was a panicked yelp and a crash of metal and Peter was down again, dangling by one leg over the edge of the bed. Still caught in that last strap.

He pushed up from the floor, writhing around, yanking violently at his trapped ankle. Kara bent down to grab him, but Peter swung out his free foot and caught her in the stomach.

Soren hesitated, taking a step towards his mum.

"No!" she demanded. "Get the others!"

He whirled around to face me again, and I ran.

Someone screamed behind me, but I barely even heard it. There was another crash of metal, but by then I was already through the surveillance room and out into the hallway.

Soren was right behind me. Some dark corner of my brain still remembered the way back to the surface and I kept going, up the hall and through another door.

"Stop!" Soren panted as I started up the dark stairs. I felt his hand scraping the back of my shirt.

I pushed on, feet hammering, hand against the wall to keep from falling over the far edge. Head throbbing. Ankles raw and screaming.

My foot caught on a bump in the mouldy concrete and I stumbled, landing hard on my knees. I pushed back to my feet, expecting Soren's hands to come clamping down any second.

But the hands never came.

I kept climbing the spiral of stairs. Dim light over my head now. The entrance. Jordan was already out.

Almost there.

And then the light started to disappear.

Soren was doing what he should have done in the first place: sealing us in.

I scrambled up on my hands and knees, watching

the sky shrink away again as a square of dirt and concrete slid out from the tunnel wall.

Just a few more steps. Too many. There was no way—

A hand shot down into the tunnel. It grabbed my arm, dragging me up and over the edge. Jordan. She let me go, sending me collapsing into the grass, and shot her arm back down through the gap.

"Peter!" she hissed into the darkness. "Peter, c'mon!"

I got up, holding on to a tree for support. "Jordan…"

"Get up here! Grab my hand!"

She leapt back, dragging her hands out a second before the tunnel closed on top of them. There was a tiny whoosh of compressed air and the square of earth slid back up into place.

Jordan sat on the grass, chest heaving. "What – *happened?"*

And suddenly the reality of it came caving in on me. "He's gone," I said. "I left him behind."

Chapter 4

For a few seconds, I just stared at the ground. Waiting for it to split open again. Waiting for them to come after us.

Then something crunched a little a way off.

I froze. For a second I'd forgotten that Kara and Soren weren't the only ones chasing us.

"Security," hissed Jordan, yanking my arm. "C'mon!"

We bolted into the trees. I looked back, didn't see anyone, kept running anyway. They were still after us. And, last I'd heard, their orders from Calvin were to shoot on sight.

The bush grew thicker up ahead. Long, spindly grass hiding a minefield of rocks and holes and tree roots. Jordan dived into the grass, dragging me down with her, and we took cover behind a towering eucalypt. I pressed myself against the base of the tree, straining to listen over the buzz of the cicadas.

I didn't hear the footsteps until they were right on top of us. A slow, heavy crunching of boots. A few metres away, maybe less.

Jordan bit her lip, grabbing my hand.

The footsteps stopped. I heard a yawn from the other side of the tree. All he had to do was take one more step, and we were dead.

The ground crunched again and I almost ran for it. More footsteps. He was moving.

He was moving *away*.

I waited until the noise died off, and sat up in the dirt, head spinning.

It was morning, sky still getting lighter, which I assumed meant we'd been down there for a day and a night. Mum had probably reported me missing by now. Or not. Maybe she'd had a late one at work last night and hadn't even realized I was gone.

"Let's go," Jordan breathed.

"But—"

"You think he's the only one out here?"

I got up and started walking, hardly believing that Shackleton wasn't still watching our every move from his office. It had been close to a month since he'd had Dr Montag put the suppressors in us, and I had to keep reminding myself that we were free to move again.

Not that we had anywhere to go. Even if Shackleton still wanted us alive – and that was pretty a massive *if* at this point – Calvin had other plans. And apparently he was willing to go behind the boss's back to see them through. There was no going back to our normal lives (or what had passed for normal in Phoenix, anyway). That was all over now.

The bushland slipped past me like it wasn't real. I was somewhere else, caught up in the twisting and churning in my stomach. In the last twenty-four hours I'd been beaten up, shot at, chased through the bush, paralysed, kidnapped and knocked unconscious – and it had all been for nothing.

We'd found Peter. He'd been *right there*.

And I'd run away.

"It's not your fault," whispered Jordan, like she was seeing into me. "There was nothing you could have—"

"I left him!" I said. "I saw him fall and I ran anyway."

"We both ran," said Jordan.

"Yeah, but you didn't—"

"What were you gonna do, Luke? Take them both on by yourself? Look at you. You're one bruise away from a coma."

"Jordan—"

"Listen," she snapped, "*I* woke them up. *I* opened the entrance before you could get him out. And then I ran off and left *both* of you, so if we're handing out blame—"

"It wasn't like that."

"It was exactly like that. It was a disaster. But when has it ever been anything else in this place?" She stopped walking, hugging herself against the cold.

"So ... now what?" I said. "I mean, we have to go back and get him, right?"

Jordan stared past me, back the way we'd come. "No. We can't. Not yet, anyway. The only way back down there is if they let us in. And they'll only do that if they know they can capture us again."

"We can't just..." I trailed off. She was right.

"We should go back into town," said Jordan.

"We can't do that either!" I said. "If Calvin sees

36

us— If anyone sees us—"

"We have to get back to our families. Let them know what's going on before they do anything to make Shackleton—"

"You want to *tell* them?" I said.

"No – not about—" She closed her eyes. "I don't know. Maybe. Maybe we have to."

"Maybe," I said. "But how happy do you think Mum's going to be when Montag's name comes up? Somehow, I don't think she's going to respond too well when I say that her new boyfriend's helping plot the apocalypse."

"Yeah, OK. Well, one thing at a time. We need to make sure they're all right, at least. We can figure out the rest as we go."

I thought about pointing out that this kind of planning hadn't exactly served us well in the past, but Jordan was looking shaken up enough as it was, and I didn't want to push it.

We headed for her place first. It was right up at the north edge of town, and we'd be able to see it from the bush.

I slowed down as a row of identical two-storey houses came into view between the trees. Jordan and I crouched again. There was a line of scraggly undergrowth in front of us, right at the edge of the bushland.

Jordan got down on her stomach, squeezing her way through the bushes for a closer look at the street. The undergrowth clawed at me as I clambered in next to her, scratching at my assorted cuts and bruises.

Jordan's place was on the corner across from us, one street parallel to the bushland and the other heading down to the town centre. Georgia's pink swing set sat on the front lawn – the only thing distinguishing their house from all the others.

Judging by the light, I guessed it was maybe eight o'clock in the morning. Already, there were people whizzing back and forth along the bike path in front of us. A couple of houses down, a guy in a suit was out watering his lawn before work.

As usual, no matter how ridiculous things got for Jordan, Peter and me, life for everyone else in Phoenix just continued as normal.

"Should be OK," said Jordan, wriggling closer to me. "We'll just wait until the traffic clears a bit, and sneak across before—"

She gasped, grabbing my wrist.

Her front door had just swung open.

A black-uniformed security guard walked out

on to the front porch. He yawned, lacing his fingers together and stretching them above his head, then leant casually over the railing.

We were too late.

Jordan's mum and dad had already been suspicious. Already dangerously close to the truth about Phoenix. They'd been trying to book a flight back home for a week now. It didn't take much imagination to see how they would have reacted when Jordan went missing.

I winced as Jordan tightened her grip on my arm. She was shaking her head at the guard, eyes dark. "If they've done *anything*…"

"There's another one," I said, trying not to think about what might be going on back at my place. The second guard was upstairs, peering out into the bush from behind a closed window.

"That's Mum and Dad's room." Jordan let go of me and started backing out from the undergrowth.

"Jordan, stop—"

"They've got my family!" she hissed.

"Yeah," I said, scrambling out after her, "and how is getting shot going to help that situation?"

She pushed to her knees. "We have to do something!"

"We have to wait until there's something we *can*

do! If they've got your family, then they've got my mum. And Peter's parents too, probably. We can't … just…"

I trailed off, seeing more movement across the street. Jordan caught it too, and we dived back under the bushes for a better look.

Her front door was opening again. The guard on the porch turned around. Jordan's mum came out, baby bump bulging, holding a mug of coffee. The guard smiled and reached out to take it from her.

Mrs Burke called back over her shoulder and Jordan's little sister, Georgia, came bounding out the door in her school uniform. Jordan's mum took her by the hand, leading her out the front gate and down the street towards school.

I glanced at Jordan. Her face was frozen, squinting across the road like she was sure there'd been some kind of mistake.

"Huh?" she managed after a bit.

"I don't think…" I began, still working it out as I spoke. "What if those guys aren't guarding your family from getting away? What if they're guarding the *house*? Maybe the Co-operative's only doing this to make sure we can't come back home."

"Then why would my parents—?" She sighed.

"Right. Because they just think security's there to help find their missing daughter."

"Well, that's kind of true," I said.

"Yeah, well, I'm assuming they left out the part about wanting to kill us." She rested her head on her hands, still watching the house. "I just hope Mum and Dad don't start asking too many—" Her brow furrowed. "Hey. Dad's still home."

I searched the windows and spotted Mr Burke's towering figure standing in Jordan's bedroom. He was slumped over, hands resting on the windowsill, and I didn't need to see the tears to know that he was crying.

I looked at Jordan, worried that she was going to jump up and start waving her arms around or something. But she just looked at him, fighting back her own tears.

"He's not going to work," she whispered. "And he's not taking Georgia to school either."

"Does that mean something?"

"He doesn't want Mum to be alone with the security officers. He doesn't trust them."

Then, as though this was the crucial detail we'd been waiting for, Jordan slid back out from under the bushes and sat up. "We need a hiding place," she said, determination blazing up again in her eyes. "Somewhere safe while we figure out what to do next."

"Safe," I repeated. I was pretty sure that no longer existed for us.

And if it did, we weren't going to find it in town. Shackleton had done a pretty slick job of turning the rest of Phoenix against us, convincing them that we were dangerous criminals. Besides, anyone who *did* help us would be putting themselves in danger, whether they knew it or not. Too many people had already wound up hurt or dead because of—

And then another possibility occurred to me.

It was dangerous, and probably stupid, and the fact that I was even thinking of it was proof of how much Phoenix had screwed with my head.

"I might know somewhere," I said. "But we'll need to wait until it gets dark."

Chapter 5

"Remember," I said, "second block, fourth house on the right, up the right-hand side, and then—"

Jordan made an impatient noise. We'd been over this at least a hundred times today.

"OK, fine," I said. "Just don't die, all right?"

"You either," said Jordan, eyes on the footpath ahead of us. *"Go!"*

We sprinted out from the bush, across one bike path and down another, weaving back and forth to stay out of the streetlights.

It was dark. Probably somewhere close to midnight.

Once the school day had started and Mrs Burke

was back from the school run, we'd moved to the east side of town, getting some distance from the last place Calvin had spotted us.

We'd spent the rest of the day watching the town from between the trees, trying to get an idea of what else security might be doing to find us now that our suppressors were gone, Jordan grumbling at least once an hour about losing her binoculars to Kara and Soren.

"Wait!" whispered Jordan, stopping at the end of the block.

I peered around the corner. A pair of security officers were coming up the cross street.

Jordan jumped the low picket fence of the nearest house. I vaulted over behind her, dropping to the grass as I heard voices out on the street.

"– gonna put their hand up for that," one of them was saying. "Not after what happened to Kern and Miller."

I pressed closer to the fence, squinting through a gap in the palings, but all I could see was grass and footpath.

"Course they will," said the other guard. "Chance to hold a weapon? Chance to play soldier? Course they'll come."

A chill cut through me as I recognised the voice.

Officer Barnett. One of the guards from out at the crater yesterday morning.

Two pairs of black boots stepped into my line of sight.

"Don't even see why we need them," said the first guard. "I know our numbers are down, but we've always had more than enough—"

"Chief's got his reasons," said Barnett.

"What do you mean?"

"I *mean*," said Barnett, voice even lower now, "Chief's got his reasons."

The other guard didn't say anything to this. His legs shifted. He was looking around. I shrank further into the fence, picturing Barnett jumping on top of me and snapping my neck. Both of them could be on us in three steps.

The other guard sighed. "All right, don't tell me."

The boots moved out of sight.

I stayed frozen in the shadow of the fence until I was sure they were well away from us, then rolled over on the grass, getting my breath back.

I sat up, glancing over the fence. "What do you reckon that was about?"

I turned to Jordan and realized I was alone on

the grass. I pulled myself up, whirling around in the darkness, but she was—

Jordan was slipping across the lawn towards me.

I gritted my teeth. "What are you *doing?*"

She put a finger to her lips, like *I* was the one taking stupid risks. "Just getting this out of the recycling," she said, holding up a battered copy of the *Phoenix Herald*.

"Of course you were," I said wearily.

I checked the street again. All clear.

"Ready?" said Jordan.

"No," I said. "Let's go."

We bolted down the block and then took a sharp right down the side of the fourth house, glancing over to make sure the lights were out next door.

I stopped at the first window. Checked behind me again. All clear.

I pushed it open, bracing myself for it to creak noisily. But of course, nothing creaks in Phoenix. The window slid silently open and we climbed inside. Into another cookie-cutter house.

45 Acacia Way.

The house next door to mine.

Theoretically, there were no empty homes in Phoenix. But, theoretically, there were no murdering superhuman homeless people either.

It had been twenty-two days. Twenty-two days since the horrific night we'd broken into the Shackleton Building and used a stolen phone to contact my dad on the outside. Twenty-two days of slowly losing hope that I would ever see him again.

Three security guards had died that night. Officer Reeve, murdered for helping us get inside. And two others who were just in the wrong place at the wrong time, mown down as they tried to keep Crazy Bill from escaping. I never even knew their names.

But I knew this house had belonged to one of them. A few days after he died, one of Mr Ketterley's maintenance teams had come around to empty out all the furniture and stuff. And apparently they'd left one of the windows unlocked, because a couple of times since then, I'd seen kids from school sneaking inside for a look.

Because there's so much to see in an empty house, I thought, locking the window shut behind us.

I leant against the wall, feeling a tiny twinge of relief creep in. We'd made it.

"This is so weird," Jordan whispered, creeping across the barren carpet.

It was like walking into my own home and finding it completely abandoned. I remembered having a

47

similar feeling every time my family moved house, when we still lived with my dad. Only back then it didn't have the constant-threat-of-death part mixed in.

I moved across to the hallway, and we started going through the place, room by room, making sure it really *was* deserted.

I felt around in the kitchen cupboards, in case Ketterley's guys had left anything edible behind. But it was like no-one had ever lived here.

We kept going. I opened the door to the ground-floor bedroom. Dim light spilled out of the room.

I panicked, slamming the door, but Jordan grabbed it before it could bang shut.

"Shh!" she hissed, pointing.

I took a second look and realized that the light wasn't shining out of the room – it was shining *in* from next door. My house.

The dining room light was on. Sitting at the table, reading a newspaper with his back to us, was a blonde-haired security officer. I backed out of the doorway and closed the door, stomach turning.

We finished searching the house. I walked out of the last bedroom and stood on the upstairs landing, staring down at the front door. Jordan leant over the railing next to me.

"We should stay here for the night," she said, keeping her voice businesslike, trying to hide all the fear and exhaustion. "Here on the landing, I mean. It's away from the windows, and we'll get at least a bit of warning if anyone comes in."

"Yeah, good idea," I said, too tired to come up with anything else.

"And we should make sure one of us stays awake," she said. "I'll—"

"I'll do it."

"Luke—"

"I'm wide awake now, anyway," I lied. "Seriously, Jordan. Sleep."

Jordan looked like she wanted to argue. But she just nodded and said, "All right. But wake me in a couple of hours, OK?"

"Yeah."

We looked at each other. And suddenly, things felt kind of awkward.

It was stupid. After all the time we'd spent alone together... But now I was going to watch her *sleep*, and I don't know why that felt so weird, but it did.

I sat on the floor and crossed my legs. Jordan lay on her side, a metre or so across from me, head resting on her arms. At first, she kept opening her eyes and looking at me, but eventually, her breathing slowed, and she slept.

I sat with my back against the railing, watching her.

And, dumb as it was, there was something calming about it, like things were OK, at least for a few minutes. I felt this sudden surge of – I don't know what. Protectiveness, I guess. Which was dumb too, because she was way more capable of looking after herself than I was. But here she was, all tired and vulnerable and – and it was just *us* now. Just her and me, at least until we got Peter back.

And I needed to step up to that.

And in that weird moment, sitting there in the cold and the dark, I actually felt like maybe I could.

Chapter 6

Saturday 27 June
47 days

I woke up, freezing, and groped around, wondering why I couldn't feel a blanket. Then I opened my eyes and remembered where I was.

"Morning," said Jordan, still sitting across from me. She was reading the newspaper.

The sun had risen, but only just, and so far it didn't seem to be helping much with the temperature.

"Hey," I said blearily, wondering how long I'd been asleep. It had still been pitch dark when Jordan had woken up and insisted on taking over the watch.

I sat up, arching my shoulders. I could see my breath in the cold air.

"Here," said Jordan, tossing me a slightly smushed chocolate bar from her pocket, wincing a bit at the movement. "Breakfast."

I ripped it open and demolished a third of it in one bite. "Thanks. How's the shoulder?"

"Fine. Wish I had another shirt to change into, though." She twisted around, showing me the patch of dried blood where Tank had smashed her with a tree branch.

Jordan opened the last chocolate bar and took a tiny bite out of the corner.

"Actually..." she said, like she was still debating whether or not to finish the sentence, "it's more than fine. I mean, it should be infected or something, right? It should've needed stitches. But look—" She grabbed her collar, pulling the shirt down over her shoulder, exposing a white bra strap and a partially-healed gash. The wound was still crusted with blood, but apart from that, it looked pretty healthy. Way better than it should have looked, not having been washed or bandaged.

"Like Calvin," I said without thinking.

"Yeah," she said, clearly not liking the comparison. "I think – I wonder whether this is connected to all the – you know—"

"X-Men stuff?" I supplied, taking another bite of my chocolate.

"Right. Like, what if the Co-operative has done this to all of us? Some kind of, I don't know, immune system boost or whatever?"

"Pretty sure they haven't given it to me," I said, taking stock of my various injuries again, all just as bad as ever.

Jordan looked thoughtful. "Yeah, but ... Montag said you weren't a genetic candidate," she said, almost apologetic, like it was some kind of club I'd been excluded from. "He said you and your mum weren't meant to be here. And maybe that's – I mean, what if that just proves what I'm saying? What if that's what a genetic candidate *is?* This – this healing stuff – what if that's what's meant to help us survive when Tabitha gets out?"

"Then I'd better hope Tabitha never gets out," I said, hearing a bitter edge in my voice.

Jordan's expression faltered. "*Luke.* Don't even— We're going to stop them. OK? That's why we're here."

I leant against the railing again, feeling the sun shine down through the skylight above my head.

That's why we're here.

Ever since Jordan had started getting her flashes of

the future or whatever they were, I'd noticed this weird new attitude creeping into the way she talked about Phoenix. Like some outside force was overseeing it all. Like there was a *point* to all this, beyond Shackleton's desire to kill everybody.

Which was a nice thought, I guess. But it's kind of hard to believe in destiny when you're hiding from your would-be killers in a dead guy's house.

Jordan took another bite of her chocolate and closed the newspaper. She glanced at me out of the corner of her eye.

"Meanwhile," she said, holding out the front page. "I think I've figured out how Shackleton can justify putting guards in our houses twenty-four seven."

I read the headline.

MURDER CHARGE FOR PHOENIX TEENS.

Underneath, a half-page photo showed Calvin and Barnett lugging a body bag out of the bush on a stretcher. The officer that Calvin had shot at the crater. And under that, three little photos of Jordan, Peter and me. The same dodgy mugshots the *Herald* used every time it had some new fake crime to accuse us of. I swore under my breath.

"Yeah," said Jordan. "Apparently, Calvin caught us trespassing out in that bushland we set fire to. Only this time, we somehow got our hands on a gun. Killed that one guard, and then injured Officer Miller when he tried to disarm us. Which, you know, doesn't make Phoenix Security look too competent, but—"

"Why do people believe this crap?" I said, snatching the paper out of her hand. "I mean, maybe the vandalism and whatever, but this is ... What is wrong with people? Seriously, how can they just swallow—?"

"Because it's easier," said Jordan, cutting into my rant. "Because the truth is complicated and scary and it would mean *not* believing a bunch of stuff that's simple and comfortable. Remember what Peter was like when we first found out about all this? Why believe there's a bigger truth out there when you can just keep your head down and tell yourself everything's OK?"

She took back the newspaper and started leafing through it again. I watched her, realizing how right she was. Realizing that was *exactly* how my mum reacted every time she was confronted with something weird in this place.

"What about your parents?" I asked. "No way are they going to believe you shot someone."

"Right," said Jordan, leaning across the paper. "Right, *but* they're still going along with Calvin's "investigation". Which means they've realized something's up, and they've realized it's dangerous enough that they don't want to make trouble."

She looked almost happy about it.

One more bite and my chocolate was gone. My stomach grumbled, like it was insulted.

"We need to eat," I said.

"Tonight," Jordan agreed. "Job number one is food – and some warmer clothes, too, if we can get them."

"Where are we going to find—?"

"Job number *two*," Jordan pushed on, holding the newspaper out again, "is figuring out what to do about *this*."

I looked down at a two-page spread about a *COMPREHENSIVE NEW SURVEILLANCE SYSTEM* that was going to *REVOLUTIONISE PHOENIX SECURITY*. It seemed like the Co-operative wasn't wasting any time turning our disappearance into an excuse to tighten its grip on the rest of the town.

The pages read like an infomercial for an exciting new product, trying to gloss over the two solid facts in the whole article: a network of outdoor surveillance cameras was being installed all over Phoenix, and it was due to go online on the first of the month.

Which meant that if we didn't have a new plan by

midnight on Tuesday, we'd be trapped in this house, waiting for the Co-operative to come and find us.

Chapter 7

I crept across the grass on all fours, along the side of yet another photocopied Phoenix home. Jordan was pulling ahead. I hurried after her.

We'd taken turns sleeping for the rest of the day. Between the stress and the exhaustion and the lack of food, I'd been too lethargic to do anything, even when I was awake. The furthest I'd moved from my spot on the carpet was a couple of trips to the upstairs bathroom.

But I was wide awake again now that it was dark, propped up by adrenalin.

We were back up at the north end of town, not

far from Jordan's place. We'd taken the long way here, slipping into the bushland and circling around under the cover of the trees, but eventually we'd had to venture back out among the houses. We'd already had a couple of near misses with security.

Jordan stopped under a low bedroom window. The light was still on inside. She turned as I reached her. "OK, get ready to run if this is the wrong bedroom."

"Wait— *What?*"

Jordan grinned and stood up. I got to my feet, peering through the window, heart thudding as I registered the good news – and the bad news.

It was the right bedroom. Lauren, the Year 7 who'd sort of befriended Jordan after she'd rescued Lauren's boyfriend from a beating a few weeks ago, was sitting on the edge of her bed, head twisted away from us.

But Lauren wasn't alone. Jeremy, the boyfriend, was right next to her, holding her face with a gloved hand, pale lips pressed awkwardly against hers.

Jordan frowned, like she didn't want to break up this beautiful moment, but then she tapped on the window and they sprung apart.

Jeremy looked like he was about to scream, and I shifted my feet, ready to run if he did.

Jordan put a finger to her lips and waved them over.

Jeremy jumped up, stepping toward the bedroom door, but Lauren said something to him and he stopped. She came over and pushed up the window.

"What are you *doing* here?" she whispered, confirming my fear that this was a bad idea. "Haven't you seen the newspaper? They're saying you shot—"

"No," Jordan interrupted, "Lauren, none of that stuff is true. You have to believe me – we would *never* do something like that."

"Obviously," said Lauren, like she'd been on our side the whole time. "What do you need?"

Jeremy stared at her like he didn't think this was *obvious* at all.

"Food," said Jordan, "as much as you can give us. Nothing perishable. And, please, make sure your parents don't—"

"Don't worry," Lauren grumbled. "They're out tonight. Meanwhile, I'm stuck babysitting my brother."

"Nice babysitting," I muttered.

Jeremy went red. Jordan punched me in the arm.

"He's in bed," said Lauren, hands on her hips. "You want my help or not?"

I held up my hands. "Sorry."

"All right, back in a sec."

She raced out of the room, Jeremy right behind her, clearly not wanting to be left alone with us.

"Did you see her mouth?" Jordan asked, when they were gone.

"Yeah," I said, leaning back to glance out at the street. The skin on Lauren's lips, and all around her mouth, had been blotchy and pale. Imprinted with Jeremy's skin tone in the places he'd touched her. The same thing had happened to Jordan's hand when she'd helped him up off the ground, back at school. "The gloves were a good idea, though."

I heard a shout from somewhere off in the distance and bobbed down into the shadows. Jordan heard it too, but only glanced over her shoulder.

Nothing to do with us.

I stood up again, leaning on the windowsill next to her.

"Must be hard," she said, eyes on the bed where the two of them had been sitting. "Trying to figure out a relationship and not even being able to touch each other."

She had this look on her face like she was talking about more than just Lauren and Jeremy, but then the bedroom door flew open again and Lauren rushed over with a shopping bag stuffed with boxes and cans. Jeremy followed, still wide-eyed.

"Thanks," said Jordan, taking the bag. "Really. Thank you so much. You're a lifesaver."

"And that's probably literal," I said, trying to make up for my comment before, mouth watering already.

"You don't have a jumper I could borrow, do you?" Jordan asked. "And, I don't know, something for Luke?"

Lauren nodded, dashing to her wardrobe.

I looked over at Jeremy.

"Sure, yeah, anything," he said frantically, pulling his hoodie up over his head. "Just please don't—"

"Wait!" I said. "This isn't—We're not *robbing* you!"

But he'd already thrown it through the window at me.

Lauren was back too, holding a black cardigan. "One of these days, you guys are going to tell me what the heck is really going on here."

"Just keep your heads down," said Jordan, putting her arm through one of the sleeves. "Don't do anything to get noticed by the Co-operative."

Another shout from the street. Closer this time.

And then a voice. "Stop right there, young lady."

Calvin. I knew he wasn't talking to us, but I stopped moving anyway.

"You never saw us," said Jordan.

"But—"

She looked at Jeremy. "And be careful with the skin thing, OK? Don't let Montag see."

Jordan shut the window and we hit the grass, back down into the shadow of the fence. I started yanking Jeremy's hoodie over my head.

"No. Get away!" called a girl's voice.

By the time I pulled my head through, Jordan was already crawling to the front of the house. I forced my arms out the sleeves and shot after her.

I could hear footsteps, but there was something weird about them. Too quick for one person, but too even for two people running together. Like a drumbeat.

And then they stopped.

We reached the front yard and ducked behind the fence. There was a girl standing out in the middle of the street. I recognized her from school. She was Korean, in the year above me, and I was pretty sure her name was Amy.

"Please," she said, edging backwards up the street, "I haven't done anything!"

She was wearing mismatched clothes – jeans, shoes, and a stripy pink pyjama top – like she'd been halfway to bed when they came for her.

"Of course you haven't," said Calvin, failing miserably at a sympathetic tone. "We're here to *help* you, Miss Park." He edged toward her, flanked by a couple of his security team.

"Get away from me!" said Amy. "I don't want your help!"

There was something not quite right about her voice. It kept shifting, fast and slow, like someone was messing with it in a computer program. Like the words were speeding up on the way out of her mouth and she had to fight to hold them back.

Calvin held up a hand, stopping the other two guards. He stepped forward on his own. "Miss Park, please, you're not well. Dr Montag is waiting to—"

He hesitated as a porch light flashed on across the street. The front door opened and a couple stepped on to the veranda. Ms Benson, our science teacher, and a guy who must have been her husband.

"Amy? Is everything all right?" Ms Benson asked. Then she caught sight of Calvin. "What's going on?"

"Back inside, please," said Calvin firmly.

"Ms Benson!" cried Amy. "They're trying to—"

"Miss Park!" Calvin barked. "Do not make this any more difficult than it needs to be."

More lights were coming on now. I saw the blinds go up in the window of another house.

She started backing away again, and I realized she had the same problem with walking as she had with speaking. Her steps were clunky, exaggerated, deliberately slow, as though moving at this speed was unnatural for her.

"Chief," Ms Benson tried again, still standing her ground, no idea how dangerous this could all get. "Amy's parents are just up the street. If you like, I could—"

Amy whirled around and *ran*.

Jordan gasped next to me.

It was like someone had hit fast-forward on the remote. Amy was halfway up the street before I even knew what was happening, quicker than any human being should be able to move.

But somehow, watching her, it was like the most normal thing in the world, as though she was the one travelling at the right speed and it was the rest of us who had a problem. All the clumsiness was gone. *This* was how she was built to move.

Calvin's men sprinted after her, but they didn't

have a chance.

More doors began to open. More people coming out to investigate. Calvin quickly put away the fury on his face, and started shooing them back into their houses.

Ms Benson backed inside, a fearful look in her eyes. Calvin was going to have a hard time covering this one up.

"I've changed my mind," I whispered. "I want them all to believe him that everything's OK."

Jordan looked at me like I'd *lost* my mind.

But if the whole point of this town was to keep us blindly going on with our lives until Tabitha was released, if it was just to make sure these last hundred days were safe and happy and peaceful...

Then what if weird stuff like this kept happening? What if people started seeing this creepy little Pleasant-ville for what it really was?

What if Shackleton decided there were more important things than keeping the peace?

Chapter 8

"Right outside my house," I said, looking through the blinds of the bedroom window. "You think they're trying to send a message?"

We were back in the empty house next door to mine. Out on the street, maintenance guys were slotting a tall, black pole into a hole in the concrete. There was a shiny half-sphere at the top, like the pole was wearing a bowler hat. And, according to the article in the *Herald*, that half-sphere had four cameras inside, feeding full three-sixty degree surveillance back to the security centre. Not that they needed it with the tag-teaming guards swarming around my house.

I dug around in the box for the last of the dry biscuits Jordan had allocated us for lunch. "Want it?"

Jordan shook her head and I shoved the biscuit into my mouth.

We'd waited in Lauren's front yard for another half-hour last night while Calvin got everyone back into their houses, then slinked back here with our bag of groceries. It turned out to be mostly biscuits, canned fruit and uncooked pasta. Not exactly a balanced diet, but at least we weren't going to starve.

Not right now, anyway.

"OK, so, three days," said Jordan, moving away from the window and pacing out across the room. "Three days until those things go online."

I waited, expecting her to follow that up with some kind of plan. But she just kept walking a slow circle around the carpet.

Because what plan was there?

Even if we did find somewhere else to hide, we'd only be buying ourselves a few more days of survival. We'd be no closer to doing anything about Tabitha. And when those cameras turned on, we wouldn't be able to *move*.

"What are we going to do about Peter?" I asked. Even with everything else that had happened in the last couple of days, the shame of abandoning him down there had never stopped gnawing at me.

Jordan stopped pacing. "What *can* we do?"

I hesitated, almost letting it drop. "Maybe we can, you know, negotiate with them. Figure out a way to—"

"You really think that's going to happen?"

Her voice wavered as she spoke, and I got the sudden feeling I was missing something. Since when was *she* the one shooting down *my* insane suggestions?

"But … we're going to have to deal with them at some point, right?" I said.

"I know," said Jordan. "I know we are. And, look, I want to get Peter back as much as you do, but—" she sighed, fingers clenching in front of her. "Even if we *could*, he's too – I mean, look at what he did to Mr Hanger. He's not *safe*. What if he blew up like that again?"

"So, what, we just leave him—?"

"They said you were going to die, Luke!"

Oh.

"What's that supposed to mean?" I asked, skin crawling.

"What do you think it means? We go back there and they're going to kill you! Look – I don't—" she stared up at the ceiling. "I don't know, OK? I don't know what we do. But we can't just—"

She staggered forward, almost crashing into me, arms dropping down to cradle her stomach.

"Jordan!"

I reached out, realising what was happening to her.

Too slow. She collapsed on her hands and knees, coughing and gagging like there was something alive inside her. Her eyes squeezed shut and I could see it was taking all she had not to cry out and give us away to the neighbours. She fell, landing in a heap on the carpet.

And then it was over.

Jordan's eyes opened. She sat up, staring around at the room, eyes sliding over me like I wasn't even there.

Because I wasn't. Not where she was.

Not *when* she was.

Jordan was having another one of her visions. Her body was still here, but she was seeing this place at some other time. At least, that was as close as she'd got to explaining it to me. And no matter how many times I saw it happen, it never stopped freaking me out.

Jordan stood up, squinting, one hand pressed to

her forehead. She turned and headed for the door, moving slowly, like she was in the dark. Which, for all I knew, she was.

I followed her on to the landing. She stopped a few steps out, looking down at the floor, taking in a scene that was apparently much more interesting than the one I was seeing. Then she crept forward again, holding the banister for support.

Jordan reached the top of the stairs and peered down. She lowered a foot on to the first step.

"No you don't," I muttered, grabbing her gently around the arms and pulling her back. "Jordan. *Jordan.* Come on, time to—"

Jordan fell back against me, shaking again. Spluttering violently. Face screwed up like she was waking from a nightmare. I stumbled back, bending to my knees, trying to lower her to the carpet before she knocked us both over.

"Hey, come on," I said, holding her still. "Come on, deep breaths. Deep breaths."

One last cough, and the shaking stopped. Jordan's eyes opened. She smirked up at me. "*Deep breaths?*"

I rolled my eyes. "What's wrong with that?"

"I'm not having a baby, Luke."

"Whatever," I grunted, pushing her off me.

"Sorry I don't have a pre-prepared list of encouraging things to say to my friend while her brain is travelling through time."

Jordan got up, rubbing her eyes.

"So what did you see?" I asked.

Her smile disappeared. "We might have a problem."

"Might?"

"It was night. I don't know when. But soon, because that was still here." Jordan gestured at our bag of food sitting against the wall. "It was scattered all over the place, though. And we were both gone. It looked like—" She turned, visualising it. "I think there might have been a struggle."

Monday 29 June
45 days

What are we still doing here? I thought, staring into the bathroom mirror. I couldn't see much in the darkness, but it *looked* like my body was finally getting to work on those bruises.

Another day gone and we were still in the house. Or I was, anyway. Jordan had sneaked out for another newspaper.

Even after her vision, she still wanted to stay here as long as we could. We had a roof over our heads, at least, and some kind of view of what was going on in the town.

Not that any of that's going to help us when Calvin comes crashing through the door.

But what else were we supposed to do? Camp out in the bush? The nights were freezing enough as it was, without—

Something flashed in the corner of my eye. My head snapped toward the doorway. A beam of light swept across the house, flickering in through the windows.

They'd found us.

I ran from the bathroom, stumbling to the bedroom at the end of the hall.

No, no, no, no—

What was I *doing* here?

I flew across to the window and stared through the blinds. Half a dozen security officers, torches in hand, semi-automatic rifles swinging from straps across their shoulders. All running. Calvin up front.

A tiny part of my brain registered that that much weaponry and manpower was probably a bit over the top, but the rest of me was too caught up in being about to die. I watched, paralysed, as they ran along the street to the front gate.

Weapons clanking. Boots pounding the concrete. And—

They kept running. Straight past the house.

I stood at the window, trying to work out why I wasn't dead yet.

Ten seconds later, they were up the street and out of sight. Slowly, it sank in. They weren't coming for us. Or if they were, they were looking in the wrong place.

I stepped back unsteadily, dizzy with relief.

A hand landed on my shoulder and I almost jumped out the window.

"Whoa – it's me!" whispered Jordan, spinning me around. She was breathing almost as hard as I was. "Did you *see* that?"

"Yeah. Where were they going?"

"I don't know," said Jordan in a rush. "Out into the bush, I think. I came out from next door and Calvin was *right there*. I was like one second away from—" She closed her eyes, shaking it off. "Anyway. It's fine. They didn't see me."

"Then who were they after?"

"I dunno. Not us." She pulled a rolled-up *Herald*

from her back pocket. "Look at this," she said, voice darkening as she shook the newspaper open.

I took it from her, holding the front page up to the streetlight glinting in through the blinds.

LOCAL YOUTH TO BE PRESENTED WITH YOUNG ACHIEVERS" AWARD.

A boy stared back from the page, his pale skin looking even more ghostly in the dim light.

"Crap," I whispered. "Jeremy."

I skimmed the first paragraph. According to the article, he'd been flown out to Canberra for some awards ceremony at Parliament House. The details were a bit sketchy – which I guess is what happens when you have to make them up in a hurry.

"Where do you think he really is?" I asked.

"Nowhere good," Jordan sighed. She grabbed back the paper and flipped it over. "It gets worse."

"Of course it does."

Usually, the back page of the *Herald* was taken up by what passed for Phoenix's sports section. Round-ups of the few local comps, plus just enough falsified details of the national rugby and cricket and whatever to keep people from getting suspicious. But today, it was dominated by a full-page ad.

A tall, muscular security officer, immaculately

dressed and airbrushed to perfection, stood against a white background, staring determinedly into the distance. Under his feet, a red Co-operative logo was stamped next to three words in sleek, bold lettering: *MAKE A DIFFERENCE.*

My stomach plummeted.

Officer Calvin was recruiting.

"It could just be making up numbers," said Jordan doubtfully. "They've already lost, what is it now, five officers? Not counting the ones in hospital."

"Could be," I said, not believing it any more than she did.

This was what Officer Barnett had been talking about the other night. Something big was coming. And whatever "difference" these guys were about to make, I had a feeling it was only going to make our lives more miserable.

Chapter 9

Tuesday 30 June
44 days

We were leaving.

I stood at one of the downstairs windows, watching the last of the sunlight melt out of the sky. I couldn't even remember coming down here. I'd been pacing all afternoon. Wandering the house, trying to walk off some nervous energy.

At midnight tonight, the surveillance cameras across the street would come online. If we wanted to get out of here, we had to do it before then.

The plan was to head out into the bush. Try to find somewhere to sleep where we wouldn't freeze to death. And then see what happened in the morning.

I left the window and went back to my pacing. It all felt so *pointless*. There was no mission. No plan. No building to sneak into, or suspect to investigate, or information to track down. It was just survival now. And what good was that if Tabitha was just going to sweep through and—

"Luke!" Jordan's voice came from above me. "Get up here!" She was leaning over the banister, waving frantically.

"What?" I said, bolting up the stairs. "What's wrong?"

She grabbed my arm, pulled me into the bedroom, and just about threw me into the window. *"Look."*

From this angle, I could see down into Mum's front lawn. Three security officers had just walked out through the front gate. They were heading up the street towards the town centre.

"So?" I said. "They're changing shifts. It's what they always do at—"

"No," said Jordan excitedly. "No, it's not! They always change over one at a time, not all at once! Luke – I think they're *going."*

I watched the guards slip out of my line of sight, and then stared down at my suddenly unguarded front lawn. The miracle that had been handed to us right when we needed it most.

There was no way it was that simple.

"Why?" I asked.

But it was like she hadn't heard me. "I'm going," she said, already halfway to the stairs. "Back to my place. If they've left your mum, then they're probably—"

I raced after her. "Jordan, just – just hang on a sec."

She turned to look at me, but I knew she wouldn't wait for long.

"What if we're doing exactly what they want us to do?" I asked.

"What do you mean? They don't know we're watching the house."

"Of course they do!" I said. "As if we wouldn't be!"

A pained look crossed her face. "Luke— What else *is* there? Our only other plan is running away."

She was right. I didn't like it, but she was right.

"I'm going," she said again. "You should too. Make sure your mum's OK."

I leant against the doorframe, wishing we had a better option. "All right," I said. "But we should meet back here. Either way, we should meet back here in a couple of hours. Figure out what to do next. We need to make sure we've still got time in case—"

"Perfect," said Jordan. "Let's go."

I followed her down the stairs. She darted into the lounge room and opened the window. She glanced up and down the side of the house, then sprung out on to the grass. I climbed out after her, sliding the window shut behind me.

I crouched down as we reached the front fence. There was a guard patrolling the next block, but he was facing the other way.

"All right," said Jordan, swinging a leg over the fence. "See you."

"Just don't—"

"Yeah," she said. "No dying. I promise."

She jogged off into the darkness.

I waited a few more seconds, glancing nervously at the security camera even though I knew it wasn't meant to turn on until midnight, then jumped over into our yard.

No point trying any of the windows. Not with Mum's obsession with keeping everything locked. I ducked across the lawn and up the steps to the front door. I peered into the frosted glass, watching for any sign of movement on the other side. Nothing. I tried the handle.

The door clicked open and I edged through, still half-expecting to find a gun barrel waiting for me.

Inside, everything was quiet. The light was on in the lounge room, further up the hall. I crept forward, trying to figure out how on earth I could explain to Mum where I'd been for the last six days.

"Mum…?" I whispered, walking in.

But the room was empty.

A couple of half-full mugs and a bunch of paperwork were spread out across the coffee table. Weird for Mum to leave work lying around like that. She didn't really do mess.

I glanced across the hall at the bathroom door, but it was wide open.

Was she even home? We'd seen her come in this afternoon, but maybe she'd left something behind at work. Maybe she'd gone back to the office to—

My gut lurched. Maybe it was a whole lot worse than that.

What if Shackleton had found out the truth about Mum not really being a candidate? What if security weren't guarding the house anymore because there was no-one left to guard?

I bolted into the hallway, through the rest of the house, checking every room for a sign of life, panic erasing the impulse to worry about keeping quiet.

No-one home.

We would've seen them, I thought desperately, sprinting upstairs. *Surely we would've seen them take her.*

On to the landing. Still nothing. Lights all off up here. I shot past my bedroom, up to the end of the hall. And stopped.

A murmur of noise from behind my bedroom door. I threw open the door without even thinking.

Oh, brilliant.

There was Mum, sitting on the edge of my bed, head down, crying into the arms of Dr Montag.

Chapter 10

**Tuesday 30 June
44 days**

Mum's eyes shot to the doorway. But if I was expecting her to jump up and hug me or something, I was out of luck. She just stared across the room at me, eyes filled with – what was that? Disappointment?

"Luke," said Montag, eyebrows raised. "Where have you—?"

And suddenly, the rage I'd been carrying around ever since he barged into our lives spewed up to the surface and I stormed over, ready to rip him to pieces.

"Get out," I spat. "Let *go* of my mum and get *out* of my house."

"*Luke,*" snapped Mum. It had been a long time

since I'd blown up like this in front of her.

"No, Mum, listen—" I said. "You can't trust him. He's dangerous."

Mum turned to stare at Montag.

She stood up, slipping out of his arms, eye make-up running down her cheeks.

"*He's* dangerous?" she choked. "After everything you've done, you're telling me *Rob* is the one I should be worried about?"

She might as well have punched me.

"Mum – none of that stuff is true! How could you even think...?" I trailed off. Mum was looking at me like she didn't know who I was.

"You've been in hiding for almost a week, Luke," said Montag, infuriatingly calm. "What are we supposed to think?"

"*Shut up,*" I hissed. "You shut up, OK? There's no *we* here! This is between me and—"

Montag held up a hand. "Luke, please."

I turned back to Mum. "*He's* the murderer!" I said, stabbing a finger at Montag. "He's the one who—"

"Luke!" Mum shouted. "Enough! I will not have you making such ridiculous accusations!"

"Yeah," I shot back, "because it would *suck* to have those flying around."

"Do you think I want this? Do you think I *want* to believe my son is capable of – of all *this?*"

"Both of you, please," said Montag, standing up and shooting me a significant look. "I think it would be wise if we all just *lowered the volume* a bit."

And for the first time since I'd walked in, he looked kind of unsettled.

Mum took a breath, gathering herself. She smoothed down the front of her jacket, brushed a tear from her cheek, and fixed me with her professional-diplomacy face, like I was just another difficult client. "All right, Luke. Tell me. What's *really* going on? Why is security after you if you've done nothing wrong?"

"Because they're—"

I hesitated, the reality of it sinking in. Because this was it. After all these weeks. After everything. I was actually going to tell her.

I glanced at Montag, but his face was blank again.

"OK, look," I said, my guts contorting. "I know this is going to sound insane, but you *have* to believe me. You have to."

Mum crossed her arms. "I'm listening."

Tell her the truth, I told myself. *She's still your mum. Just tell her the truth.*

"All right," I began. "Phoenix is – it's not what you

think it is. The Co-operative didn't bring you here to *work* for them. They brought you here because they want to, like, restart society or something. They've got a weapon, this virus thing, and in a few weeks, they're going release it and then everyone outside of Phoenix is going to die."

Silence.

Mum stared back, and the tears started rolling down her face again. "Luke…"

Please. Please…

She took another unsteady breath, and I felt my hopes rise just the tiniest bit, because if she was with me, if she was on my side, then at least…

At least…

"Oh, Luke," she said, head shaking. "Is that really the best you can do?"

It was like someone had carved a hole in my chest.

"You want proof?" I said, anger rising again. "You want to see the scar where *he*—?"

"Luke, that's enough," Montag cut in. "Why don't you go and have a shower?"

It was such a ridiculous request that I lost track of what I was saying.

"What?"

"I think we all need a minute to calm down," he

said, walking over and taking the towel from the hook on my door. "And by the look of things, you could use one. Why don't you go and clean yourself up while we head downstairs and get some dinner sorted out? Then we'll all sit down and figure this out together."

And it was so close to the kind of calm, rational suggestion my dad would have made that I almost punched him.

But Mum was already over at my wardrobe, pulling out a change of clothes.

Montag leant in, handing me the towel. The unsettled look was back. "If you care *at all* about your mother," he breathed, "you will do what I tell you."

He straightened up as Mum came back.

I was torn between screaming at her and trying to explain again and running for the door.

But in the end I just took the clothes and the towel and headed for the bathroom.

The water had still been on in the house next door, but neither of us had wanted to risk having a shower. Six days without a wash or a change of clothes.

I closed the door behind me and had to remind myself it was OK to switch the lights on. I spun the taps, stepped in, and watched the dirty water swirling around my feet.

I felt sick. Mum and I had never exactly seen eye to eye about Phoenix, but I guess I'd always figured there was a limit to it. That when it came down to it, when it really mattered, she'd believe me and not the lies the Co-operative was feeding her.

But why trust your own son when you can blindly follow a guy you've just met?

I stood there, dazed, hot water running over me and down the drain and never reaching the numbness in my chest.

She thinks you're a killer.

I wanted to stay there forever, to just disappear down that drain and forget about all of it. But eventually, the water ran cold and I dragged myself out. I dried off, pulled on the clean clothes, and stepped into the hall.

Montag was waiting just outside the door. He held up my school backpack. "You need to go now, Luke."

"Where's my mum?" I asked, pushing past him.

"She's gone. I sent her into town to pick up some dinner. Security will be back in half an hour. You need to—"

"Screw you! You think you can just come in here and—?"

"Do you want her to die?"

88

Montag took me by the shoulder, fingers digging into my skin. "Mr Shackleton has already asked me for your blood test results. He wants to hand them over to Dr Galton so she can conduct a threat assessment. Apparently, he feels that my relationship with your mother may be impeding my objectivity. I've tried to stall him, switched your mother's sample and told him yours was contaminated during that debacle with Peter in the school gym, but if you get caught…"

Then Shackleton will have all the blood he wants.

And if Shackleton and Galton got their hands on another sample of my blood, they'd have no trouble figuring out that Mum and I weren't supposed to be here. We'd be as good as dead.

Montag relaxed his grip on me, shoving the backpack into my chest. "Go."

I stood, frozen, hating him for poisoning Mum against me, for *taking* her from me. For sending me out of my own house while he stayed behind and played wounded stepdad.

But I knew he was right, that this was my only chance at keeping her safe.

I walked away from him, leaving the backpack dangling in his hands, and crossed to my bedroom. A couple of photos of Dad and me were stuck up on the wall. The only ones I had. I pulled them off and put them in my pocket, wishing it had been him and not Mum out here all this time.

"You'll lose her," I said, coming back and yanking the bag away from him. "Doesn't matter what happens to me. It's all going to come out eventually."

Montag nodded grimly. "I'm beginning to think you're right."

"Yeah, well, I just hope I get to see it happen."

I took off down the stairs. I was halfway across the front yard when something snapped inside my head.

Jordan.

The security officers had only left my house because Montag wanted some alone time with Mum. They'd still be all over Jordan's place.

I sped up, jumping the fence into the next yard and racing around to the far side of the empty house, making sure Montag wouldn't see me going in.

She'll be fine, I told myself. *She won't go running in there without looking.*

But if there was one sure-fire way to make Jordan do something reckless, it was putting her family in danger.

I threw open the dining room window and dived inside, trying to think. If anything happened to her...

90

I'd already lost Mum tonight. I couldn't lose Jordan too.

I ran to the stairs and almost shouted as my foot collided with something solid. I bounced on one leg, looking back to see what I'd just kicked, and saw a dark shape rolling away across the floor.

One of the big fruit tins that Lauren had packed for us.

How——?

Jordan's vision. Food scattered everywhere.

What if security had seen her? What if they'd followed her back here?

I grabbed the banister and limped to the top of the stairs, pain still shooting through my foot.

More cans and boxes strewn across the floor. Every-thing quiet. "Jordan?"

I picked up another one of the big tins. Not much of a weapon, but better than nothing, if I was about to walk in on someone. I started toward the nearest bedroom. "Jordan?"

"Luke!" And then I heard her grunt, like she'd just been punched in the gut.

I headed for the room at the end of the hall, a lump in my throat. A figure stepped into the doorway, blocking my path. Not a security guard. A wiry, dark-haired boy with one arm in a sling. Mike.

He smirked at the look on my face. "Come on, man. Did you really think the overseers would let you off that easy?"

Chapter 11

"Let her go," I said, brandishing the fruit tin at him.

Mike whipped out his uninjured hand. "Drop it."

He was clutching a nasty-looking kitchen knife.

"Whoa – Mike – Come on—"

"*Now,*" said Mike, hand twitching. He was shaking a bit, but I could see that he meant business.

"OK. *OK!*" I stepped back, dropping the tin.

He glanced over his shoulder. "Cat!"

Urgent whispers from the next room, and then Cathryn walked out with a reel of fishing line. Jordan stumbled after her, wrists tied together, Tank shoving her along with both hands. She started to say something, but he punched her in the back. "Shut up."

"Arms out in front of you," Mike ordered.

"Mike, seriously, just—"

"This is not a freaking negotiation, Luke!" He swung the knife around again, aiming it at Jordan. "Just shut up and do what you're told or I'll cut her open."

I put out my arms. Cathryn came over and looped my wrists together with the fishing line. She was shaking even worse than Mike. Refusing to make eye contact.

Cathryn pulled the line tight between my wrists, knotting it together. Mike bent down to inspect her work, then cut it from the reel.

"All right," said Mike, gesturing down the stairs with his knife. "Time to go."

"Where are you taking us?" I asked.

Mike slammed a foot into my shin. "Move."

Cathryn shoved me forward. We stumbled down the stairs, her and me in front, then Mike, Jordan and Tank.

Mike overtook us as we reached the front door. He walked out and scanned the street. "OK," he said, turning around. "Down to the front gate, and then we run. *No stopping* until we hit the bush."

"I'm not running anywhere," said Jordan.

"Really?" Mike raised the knife again, pointing it at her chest. "You sure about that?"

"Do it, then," said Jordan. "How happy do you think your *overseers* are going to be if you don't bring us back to them in one piece?"

"You know what?" said Mike, obviously working hard to keep his voice steady. "They didn't actually specify the number of pieces they wanted."

I flinched as he switched targets, stabbing the knife back in my direction.

"So how about you just keep moving before somebody gets hurt?"

They marched us down the steps to the front gate.

"Ready?" said Mike, checking the street again. "OK. *Now!*"

We ran, straight up the middle of the road, not even bothering to avoid the streetlights. Jordan pulled ahead, dragging Tank along behind her, until she was level with Cathryn and me. She caught my eye, shot me a *get ready* look—

And dropped to the ground.

Tank swore as he lost his grip and went flying into the path. Cathryn stopped running and spun around. I threw myself forward, twisting my shoulders. She let go of me and I doubled back for Jordan, who was already halfway to her feet.

But then Mike swooped in behind her, bringing his good arm up around her neck, blade hovering at her ear. Jordan gritted her teeth. "You don't want to try that again," growled Mike, yanking her the rest of the way to her feet. "*Tank*. Get over here."

Tank got up and took hold of Jordan again.

"Seriously man," said Mike, using his knife arm to untangle his sling, "I give you one job to do…"

"Sorry," Tank grunted. "She was—"

His mouth slammed shut as a porch light flashed on across the street.

"Crap!" hissed Mike. "Go, go, go!"

Cathryn shoved me up the road and we bolted. Through the streets and into the bush, not stopping until the lights of the town were completely blocked out by the trees.

Mike slowed down, panting, and we fell into line behind him. He stabbed his knife off to our left. "This way."

"The lake?" Jordan asked.

"Shut up," said Tank.

But she was probably right. If past experience was anything to go by, these guys had been ordered to dump us somewhere for Kara and Soren to come and pick up. Somewhere familiar, I was guessing, and I doubted they'd go for the crater again.

We pushed on, eyes slowly adjusting to the dim moonlight. I shivered, regretting the shower I'd had, cold damp hair sticking to the back of my neck.

Cathryn sniffled behind me. Jordan glanced over.

"I'm sorry," Cathryn whispered, and I could tell from her voice that she was on the verge of tears. "I'm sorry. It's the only way."

"*Cat*," Mike warned.

"The only way to do *what?*" said Jordan.

Tank hit her again. "I said shut up."

But then Jordan made a noise like she'd figured it out on her own. "Peter," she said. "A trade? Is that what they offered you?"

"The overseers don't make *offers*," Mike snarled. "They tell us what to do, and we do it."

"They won't give him to you," said Jordan.

Cathryn faltered, pulling me to a stop. "They will."

"Cathryn, we've *met* them. They're not what you think they are."

Mike whirled around, knife in the air again. "You are going to close your freaking mouth *right now*, or

97

I'll cut you a new one."

But now Tank had stopped too. He turned Jordan around, holding her out at arm's length. "What are you talking about?"

"None of it is real!" said Jordan. "All of that destiny stuff. The tattoos and the candles and – they're just *people*. They're *using* you. There's nothing—"

Jordan broke off, screaming, as Mike stabbed the knife into her arm. She doubled over, trying to bring her bound hands up to put pressure on the wound, but it was too close to her elbow.

Cathryn reeled back, horrified. "What is your *problem?*"

"I warned her," said Mike, staring down at his hands. "I warned her…"

I lunged at him.

He thrust the knife at me. "You want one too?"

"Mike, *stop!*" Cathryn shrieked, trying to push between us.

Jordan was hunched over against a tree, gasping in pain. There was a ragged hole in her sleeve, but it was too dark to see how bad the cut was.

"All of you – KEEP MOVING!" roared Mike. He turned to Tank, looking slightly insane now. "If they're not at the lake by ten—"

"Mate, hang on a second," said Tank. He turned back to Jordan. "Using us for *what?*"

Mike's eyes bulged. "TANK! We don't have time for a bloody Q and A here! Hurry up and—"

A light shot out from the bushes, straight into Mike's face.

"Whoa! Hey! No!" I shouted, panic sweeping over me. "Don't shoot!"

The light darted away from Mike, hitting me square in the chest.

Jordan pushed off from her tree. "Run!"

"Wait!" croaked a man's voice.

There was a crash of leaves and he staggered out. Just a silhouette at first. Ragged beard, unbrushed hair. He stopped a few paces away. His torch hovered over me for a second longer. Then he swung it around, lighting up his own face.

And I stared back at him.

And I stared.

And the whole world fell out from under me.

"Dad?"

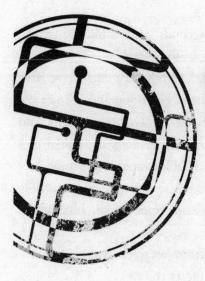

Chapter 12

Tuesday 30 June
44 days

"Luke…" Dad smiled, tears in his eyes, looking like he didn't believe it any more than I did, and I realized just how big a part of me had actually believed he was dead.

I was still too stunned to move when Mike sprang forward. "Back into the bushes, old man," he warned, aiming the knife up at Dad's face. "Just turn around."

Dad flinched the slightest bit, then brought his hands up. "Put it down, kid."

"Yeah, Mike," said Tank. "This isn't what we came here for."

"You think I won't do it?" said Mike, becoming

more and more unhinged as he lost control of the situation. "You think I won't—?"

Dad's hand shot out at Mike.

Mike jumped back, slashing the knife through the air. Dad reeled back, swung out his other hand, and caught Mike around the wrist. The knife jerked to a stop, centimetres from Dad's chest.

I was shaking. It was all creeping past me in slow motion, but my brain wasn't absorbing any of it.

He was *right there*.

Mike shouted, twisting the blade around, trying to cut Dad anywhere he could reach. Dad dropped his torch and used his other hand to pry the knife away.

I fumbled for the torch, my hands still stuck together. By the time I'd straightened up again, Dad had the knife at his side and Mike was edging away, looking murderous.

Dad dropped the knife and stood on it. "You need to go now."

"Tank!" yelled Mike, almost hysterical now. "Get the fishing line!"

Tank shook his head. "Mate, it's over."

"It *will* be over if we don't—!"

"Listen, kid," Dad stepped forward and grabbed

Mike by the shirt. "You just threatened my boy with a kitchen knife, which makes you *extremely* fortunate to still only have one broken arm. Believe me when I tell you that walking away is your *best* option right now."

Mike glared at Dad. "Screw you." But he pulled out of Dad's grip and turned away, rejoining Cathryn and Tank.

They disappeared into the bush.

Dad picked the knife up and started cutting my hands free. "Who was that?" he asked.

I didn't answer. I'd heard him, but not the words. Just his voice.

His voice.

He was alive.

The last thread of fishing line snapped apart and my hands came loose. I looked up into his dirty, unshaven face, and he was still there, still *real*, and I reached out, pulling him into a crushing hug.

His arms came down around my back and I just fell apart. I clung on to him like a little kid, terrified that this time was going to be the same as all the others, that I'd wake up and realize it was all just in my head.

"My boy..." he sniffed, pulling me in even tighter. "It's OK... It's OK..."

A pained grunt from the darkness snapped me out of it.

"Jordan!" I let go of Dad. "Sorry. Sorry, I was…"

She smiled. "No worries."

"She's hurt," I said. "Her arm. Do you have anything?"

"Wait. Not yet," said Jordan. "We're making too much noise. We need to get away from here."

I glanced at the dark blotch on the arm of her jumper.

"We'll get worse than this if security find us," she said, catching me looking at her. "C'mon."

We pushed on for a few minutes, deeper into the bush. Eventually, Jordan stopped at a massive fallen tree, sat down, and stretched out her arms so Dad could cut her free.

Dad shrugged off a worn-out old backpack and handed it to me. "There should be a couple of bandages in there somewhere."

I zipped open the bag and shone the torch inside. Dirty clothes, a couple of half-empty water bottles…

"How did you *get* here?" asked Jordan, her arms unbound now, taking off her jumper for a better look at the wound. "The night we called you, Shackleton – the guy in charge here – he was going to trace our call and send some of his guys out to, you know, *deal* with you."

"Yes," Dad said darkly. "He did. Thankfully, I wasn't home when you called. I was in Melbourne on business. They came to the hotel. But there was a conference on, and by then the morning crowd was up." He breathed a long sigh. "I got away."

"Here," I said, finally finding the bandages. I handed Dad one of the little white rolls and flashed the torch on to Jordan's arm. There was blood everywhere.

I went back to Dad's bag for a water bottle. Jordan flinched as I poured the water out over her arm, washing away the blood.

"It doesn't look too bad," said Dad, examining the gash. "It could do with a few stitches." He glanced up, catching my eye. "But that's not an option, is it?"

I shook my head. "We're not very popular with the doctor right now."

Dad stretched out the end of the bandage and started wrapping it around Jordan's arm.

"So you got away from Shackleton's guys..." Jordan prompted.

"Yeah," said Dad. "I tried going to the police, but all I had was a couple of unidentified stalkers and a rumour of trouble in a town that – as far as the rest of the world is concerned – doesn't even exist. I guess I can't really blame them for being unconvinced."

I was settling down enough by now to start taking in the details of what he was saying, but it still took me a second to see what it meant.

"So … they're not coming," I said. "The police or the army or whoever. This isn't – we're not getting rescued?"

"No." Dad gave me the same sad, defeated look he used to get whenever Mum would end an argument by storming out of the house. "No, it's just me."

That should have disappointed me more than it did. But right now, "just him" felt like plenty.

"Anyway," Dad went on, "I left the police station. Took a cab straight to Melbourne Airport. It was a public place and – well, your mum could never even get a *nail file* into the terminal, so I thought I'd be at least a bit safer there. I called Dorothy from a courtesy phone. Our neighbour," he added, for Jordan's benefit. "And she told me a couple of "repairmen" had arrived at the flat that morning. I put two and two together and figured it wasn't safe to go back home."

"It's still out there," Jordan marvelled, as Dad fastened the bandage. "The world. It's still…"

"Yeah. For now." I slipped off my own backpack, which had somehow managed to stay with me this whole time, and took out another jumper. "Here, you want one that doesn't have blood all over it?"

"Thanks," said Jordan, pulling it over her head. She looked at my dad. "You don't have the time, do you?"

He glanced at his watch. "Almost nine-thirty."

"Good," she said, in the voice that always meant whatever was coming next *wasn't* good. "Plenty of time."

"Plenty of time for what?"

Jordan stood up. "We're going to go and get Peter back."

"Seriously? *Now?* But you were the one who—"

"That was before they gave us the advantage."

I didn't even bother responding to that one.

"Look," said Jordan, "they're still dangerous. I know they are. But there are three of us now. And we need a place to stay, right? You really think we're going to get another chance to catch them above ground?" She started moving off, not even looking back to see if I was coming. "The overseers want us at the lake by ten? We'll be there. And we'll be ready for them."

106

Chapter 13

"This is a bad idea," I whispered.

"No worse than usual," said Jordan. "Shh!"

It was just past 10 p.m. We were lying in the grass at the edge of the lake, opposite the creepy, candle-filled cave we'd discovered a couple of weeks back. Waiting for Kara and Soren to arrive. Hoping security didn't beat them to it.

I tried to tell myself that Jordan was right. I mean, I still didn't think this was a *good* plan, but it made at least as much sense as freezing to death out in the bush.

Dad was crouched in some bushes a couple of

metres away. I kept turning my head, making sure he was there, still not quite believing it.

"*Luke,*" whispered Jordan. "Stay *still.*"

"Sorry," I murmured, staring back up at the stars, arms behind my back so Kara and Soren would think they were tied.

In the last half-hour, we'd filled Dad in on the various people in Phoenix who were trying to kill us, and he'd given us the rest of the story of how he'd got here.

Dad had used work connections to track down some old financial documents linking Shackleton to Remi Vattel, and then used that to figure out where we were. He'd chartered a flight as close as he could get to Phoenix – the Co-operative had somehow got the 20km around the town marked out as a no-fly zone – and then made the rest of the trip on foot.

But the craziest part was how he'd got inside. On Monday night, he'd reached the giant wall that surrounded this place (which I guess explained that troop of security commandos we'd seen stomping off into the bush). He'd circuited the wall and pretty much given up hope of finding a way inside, when he spotted a rope dangling down the over the edge.

The rope *we'd* thrown over the wall six weeks ago,

on the night we'd first discovered it.

Which was almost impossible enough to make me think Jordan was right about there being some kind of purpose to all of this.

Dad had spent the last forty-eight hours sneaking through the bush, avoiding security, trying to find us.

I hadn't told him about Mum and Montag. Not yet.

I glanced over at the bushes again.

"*Stop*—" Jordan began.

Then something white moved across my peripheral vision and I dropped my head back down into the dirt. They were here.

A torch flashed on and I closed my eyes, listening to their footsteps crunching through the undergrowth. The torch beam fell on my face and I had to force myself not to squint away from it.

A foot came down next to me. Close enough to kick dirt into the back of my hand.

"They are both unconscious," said Soren in his weirdly stilted voice, crouching as he spoke.

"Mm," said Kara, unconvinced, from Jordan's other side. "Sedate them anyway."

I cringed, seconds away from—

A rustle in the bushes.

Shifting feet, and a gasp from Kara.

"*Stop*," said Dad, flicking his own torch on.

I opened my eyes. Soren was hovering over me, auto-injector pen in hand. Back in his white lab coat.

He twitched, realizing I was awake. I grabbed his wrist and he dropped the pen. His other hand came around to—

Whumph!

Jordan dived forward, tackling him, shouting at the impact to her injured arm.

Kara was standing with her back to me, eyes on Dad, who was holding Mike's knife out in front of him. Not that he would ever use it, but between the bloodied weapon and the raggedy beard, he was pretty convincing as a crazy psycho.

Jordan had Soren pinned to the ground by now, her good hand splayed across his chest. Soren gazed at her for a second, mesmerised. He reached for her hand, but Jordan thumped him hard on the chest.

Soren yelped. I felt around in the darkness, grabbed the auto-injector pen, then got up to help Jordan haul him to his feet. He flinched at the touch, made one last attempt to wrench free, then gave up and turned his attention to Dad. His face twisted as he got a better look at him. "It's the father!"

"I *know* who it is," said Kara impatiently.

"But – he isn't—"

Splash!

I whirled around, searching for whatever had just hit the water behind us.

"*Moron!*" hissed a voice from the shadows.

Kara shone her torch down to the edge of the lake. "Out," she demanded. "Where I can see you. *Now.*"

More rustling bushes, and Mike appeared. He looked petrified. Even worse than when Calvin had caught him down in the crater. Cathryn and Tank followed him out. Tank's right leg was dripping wet.

"Kneel," Kara ordered.

Mike dropped to his knees, eyes down. Tank glanced uncertainly at Kara for another second, then followed suit. Cathryn stood behind them, scared but unmoving.

"Are you kidding?" said Jordan. "Get up!"

"*Kneel!*" Kara boomed.

Cathryn dropped down to join the others.

I didn't know whether to laugh or feel sick. I could understand fear. I could understand following orders. But this was something completely different.

"No, *stop*," said Jordan, exasperated. "Look at them! Look at what's in front of you! They're just *people*."

111

"How dare you disobey a decree of the overseers?" shouted Kara, drowning her out again, still managing to sound commanding, even with Dad's knife trained on her.

"We tried!" said Tank shakily. "But then that guy came and attacked us!"

I looked over at Dad, but he didn't respond. He was watching the scene unfold, waiting before he did anything. The same steady, patient way of dealing with conflict that always used to drive Mum nuts.

"You have failed us," spat Soren, pulling against Jordan and me again. His constant twitchiness made him much worse at the whole evil overlord act than his mum, but Mike still swallowed every word.

"Please!" he said, head down in the dirt. "We did everything we could!"

"You have beheld the face of the overseers," said Kara darkly.

"No!" said Tank. "No – we weren't—!"

"Perhaps you thought you could deceive us," said Kara. "Perhaps you thought yourselves *above* the position you had been entrusted with?"

Mike dropped even lower. "No … no…"

It was insane. We had them. Soren caught and Kara looking down the wrong end of a knife. But it was like Mike and the others couldn't see any of that. Like whatever was going on in their heads was more important than the reality in front of them.

They weren't just *devoted* to their overseers. They'd been completely brainwashed.

"Enough!" shouted Jordan, staring down at Mike. "Get up!"

"Don't," Kara warned.

"Cathryn," Jordan pushed on, "you said you were *finished* with this!"

Cathryn shook her head. "I couldn't … I couldn't just leave him…"

"Quiet!" said Kara. "One more word and you will never see Peter again."

"You really think they're going to give him to you?" said Jordan.

"They're the overseers, you moron!" said Mike, like that was an answer.

"Overseers of *what?*" I said. "What does that even mean?"

"It means they do what we tell them," sneered Soren.

"Why?" said Jordan, still looking down at Mike. "Because they stuck a bunch of candles in a cave and said you had a destiny? Mike, they can't even figure out who they're meant to be fighting against!"

"That will do!" said Kara, eyes flashing.

"Yeah," said Jordan, letting go of Soren. "It will."

She yanked the auto-injector pen out of my hand and jammed it into the side of Soren's arm. He yelled out, pulling against me, almost dragging us both over as he jerked the needle back out.

Cathryn looked up.

"Eyes on the ground!" Kara ordered.

Cathryn ignored her. She grabbed hold of a low-hanging branch, pulling herself shakily to her feet.

Soren was still shouting and flailing, the same startled-animal movements. I let go of him and he staggered over to his mum, arm hanging limp by his side.

"There!" said Jordan, thrusting a hand at him. "Be-hold your invincible overseer! Pretty impressive, huh?"

Soren crumpled at Kara's feet as the sedative took over. By now the others were watching too. Dawning comprehension on Tank's face. Cold fury on Mike's.

Kara shot a piercing look at Jordan, but didn't open her mouth again. Soren let out one last muffled groan and stopped moving.

"You killed him!" said Tank, awed.

Jordan rolled her eyes. "He'll wake up in a few hours."

Mike got to his feet, pulling the sling back over his shoulder. He looked ready to rip Jordan apart.

"You really want to try it, Mike?" said Jordan. "You couldn't take me when you had *both* hands. How do you think—?"

He charged at her.

Dad stepped forward, moving between them before Mike could touch her.

"I think you children had better go," said Dad. "*All* the way home this time."

Mike looked at the knife in Dad's hand, swore at him, and turned away. And for the second time that night, the three of them slipped off into the shadows.

Dad's eyes shifted to Kara, then down to Soren's collapsed form, then back over to Jordan and me, with a look on his face like his brain was pretty close to overload.

"So," he said, "this is what you've been doing for the last two months."

"Pretty much," I sighed, rubbing my wrist where Soren had grabbed me. "And you haven't even met the *real* bad guys yet."

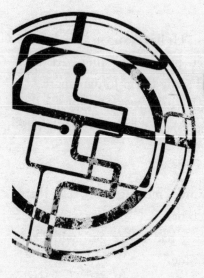

Chapter 14

**Tuesday 30 June
44 days**

"How did you find us, anyway?" I asked Kara, my voice low as we crept through the bush toward the Vattel Complex. "I mean, if the Co-operative didn't know where we were, how did you guys figure it out?"

Kara just kept walking, eyes forward. She hadn't spoken since we left the lake.

Jordan made a frustrated noise behind her. "What, the mighty overseer can't answer a simple question?"

No response.

We kept moving, torches off. Dad was next to me, carrying a still-unconscious Soren. He grunted, shifting him across to his other shoulder.

116

A few more steps and we came to the bike path. Somehow, I'd ended up out in front. I looked both ways, and dashed across to the other side, where a line of black Shackleton Co-operative security tape still marked out a wide stretch of bushland around the crater.

"What's this?" Dad asked.

"Long story," I said. "C'mon."

We stepped over. Not far to go now.

But there's still time for security to find us, I thought.

"It's sick," said Jordan. "You know that, right?" I looked back and realized she was talking to Kara again. "Twisting people's minds around. Wanting to be worshipped. That's, like, an actual illness."

No response.

"How long did it take you?" Jordan asked, voice rising. "Stroking their egos, telling them they were *special.* How long did it take you to break them down like that?"

"Don't even bother," I said. "She's not—"

"They believed in you!" Jordan raged. "They risked their lives because you made them think they were part of something!"

"They *were* part of something!" Kara shot back, finally cracking.

"They could have been killed!"

"Yes," said Kara. "Three lives weighed against the whole of humanity."

"You're not helping humanity!" Jordan seethed. "And they weren't your lives, were they? You were safe and sound, down in your little—"

"*Shh!*" I said, turning back. "Just— Look, just wait till we get down there, OK? We can't do this out here."

Jordan dropped back again. "Yeah. Sorry."

We walked the rest of the way in silence.

I thought about Mike, Cathryn and Tank, kneeling in the dirt at the edge of the lake. They'd kidnapped Peter, tied us up at knifepoint, slashed Jordan, beaten me up, and almost got us both gunned down by Calvin and his men, all because they'd been dumb enough to buy into a bunch of crap from Kara and Soren about it being their *destiny*.

So how come I was suddenly feeling sorry for them?

We marched Kara down through the long, reedy grass and into the dense bushes toward the Vattel Complex. Still no sound except for our crunching footsteps and a few night animals.

I slowed down, straining to make out a low, dark

shape running though the dirt in front of me. The decaying remains of a concrete wall. Part of whatever this place used to be, back before Phoenix.

I crossed to the tunnel entrance. Dad sent me a puzzled look.

"Well?" I said, looking to Kara.

She didn't move.

"You really want to still be out here when the sun comes up?" said Jordan.

Kara's lip curled. She pushed her lab coat aside and pulled something from her back pocket. I flicked Dad's torch on, flashing it down on her hand. She was holding what looked like a straightened-out paperclip with a lump of plasticine or something on the end.

Kara bent down at another ruined wall and pushed the grass aside to reveal two little holes, side by side in the concrete. I thought back to Pryor's office and realized those holes had probably once had a power outlet in front of them. Kara stuck the end of the paperclip into one of the holes and dug it around inside for a second. There was a sharp hiss, and the tunnel entrance started sinking down into the ground.

"Huh," said Dad in surprise.

Kara pocketed the paperclip again, looking extremely unimpressed at being forced to give away this secret. She moved to head inside.

Jordan grabbed her by the back of her coat. "Why don't you let me go first?"

She brushed past, down into the tunnel. Kara followed after her.

"Make sure you keep to the left," I told Dad, stepping in. "It spirals down, and there's no railing on the— Oh, no."

Torches flickering through the trees. Not close enough to reach us, but they would be soon.

Dad and I dropped into the tunnel.

"Security!" I called down into the darkness. "Quick, how do we close it up?"

"There's a button on the wall," Kara called back. "Level with the third step."

I scratched at the mouldy concrete. "I can't—"

"Got it," said Dad, and the concrete-and-dirt slab started sliding back into place.

I bounded down the steps, heart smashing against my chest, not even breathing until the last glint of moonlight had disappeared.

I reached the bottom of the tunnel, glancing back to check that Dad was still there. We headed through the door and joined Jordan and Kara in the dirty hallway, already mid-argument.

"You're not taking him," said Kara.

Jordan ignored her, heading through to the room with all the surveillance computers.

I pushed open the door to Soren's bedroom. Dad dropped Soren off, and we hurried to catch up with the others.

"You *can't*," said Kara, striding in behind Jordan. "You have no idea what he's—"

Jordan turned to face her. "You want proof that we've got nothing to do with this? Fine. We can give it to you. But we need Peter to get it."

We do?

An explosion of jangling metal rang out from the next room. Peter was straining against his bed again.

"Jordan!" he called. "Jordan – in here!"

Jordan crossed the room, into the laboratory place. Kara shot after her.

I scanned the surveillance computers on my way past, checking for security guards up at the entrance. A guard shot straight across the path of the camera and kept running.

Good.

"Through here," I said, glancing at Dad again.

But Dad was fixated on the wall behind me, eyes drifting over the creepy serial-killer pin boards that showed just how long Kara and Soren had been trying to track us down. He stretched out a hand, brushing the face of one of my old primary school photos.

Why us? I wondered again. Where were they getting their information from?

"What *is* this place?" Dad asked.

"Yeah, good question," I sighed. "Come on. Better make sure Kara doesn't try anything."

As we walked through to the next room, I noticed a printer in the corner near the door, with a few sheets of paper lying on top. My own face stared back at me from the first page. A blurry black-and-white image, probably scanned from a newspaper article. I picked up the papers and took them with me into the lab.

We came through the door and found Kara standing with her back to Peter's bed, trying to keep Jordan from getting to him. Peter was still thrashing against his restraints, looking determined to destroy Kara even if he had to bite her to death.

"Peter!" Jordan shouted. "*Calm down.* We're going to get you out."

Peter stopped struggling, but there was no change in the rage on his face.

I ran around to the other side of the bed. Kara's eyes darted back and forth between Jordan and me.

"Get away from him," I said.

Dad dropped the knife into one of the sinks along the wall and came across to join us, taking Kara by the arms and pulling her away from Peter.

"Please," she said, looking up at Dad, desperation slipping into her voice now. "Please believe me. This is a mistake."

Jordan was already pulling back the belt from across Peter's still-bandaged head. I left the papers and the torch on the end of the bed, and reached over to start on his ankles.

"Sure you don't have somewhere else to run off to, mate?" he asked, and I felt the shame well up again.

"Peter, listen, I'm *really* sorry about—"

"You left me!" he shouted, stretching up as another strap came away.

I backed away, just in case. "Sorry! I'm sorry, OK? It was an accident."

"Yeah," said Peter. "I hate it when I accidentally run up a bunch of stairs."

"Listen," hissed Jordan, "we almost died that night! We almost got shot trying to find you. So just drop the attitude, all right? We're getting you out."

Peter's face flashed with regret. "No, I didn't mean..."

123

He slumped back down to the bed.

Jordan moved around to free his wrist, and Peter shot a covert little snarl at me behind her back, like it was *my* fault she'd defended me. He wasn't making it easy to keep feeling sorry for him.

Peter looked over at Dad, like he'd just noticed him. "Crazy Bill has a brother?"

"That's my dad." I stepped forward cautiously, loosening the strap from his leg.

"No, seriously. Who is it?"

"It's true," said Jordan. "He got here last night."

Peter pulled a face like he still didn't know whether to believe it. "Where have you guys been, anyway?"

"Hiding out in town," said Jordan, getting his other leg undone. "Trying to find a safe way to get you out of here. Good thing these guys got rid of our suppressors, otherwise we never would've—"

"No they didn't," said Peter, sitting up.

Jordan looked up. "Sorry?"

"How do you reckon they knew where to send Mike to get you?"

"But we've been up there almost a week, and Calvin never even—" I broke off, suddenly getting it. I turned to Kara. "You didn't take them *out* of us. You just – what? Reprogrammed them or something?"

"Clever boy," said Kara dryly.

They'd been tracking us the whole time. Just waiting for a chance to send Mike and the others out to pick us up.

"Probably reconfigured the tracking signals to attack Shackleton's computer and erase our positions," said Peter. "That's what I would've done, anyway. Shackleton must've been distracted when it happened though, or else—"

Jordan whipped around, face to face with Kara again. "*Take them out.*"

"No," said Kara.

"I don't really think you're in any position to refuse," said Dad, still holding tight to both of her arms.

I shook my head, amazed at his ability to just pick up all of Phoenix's weirdness and run with it. Like all of this was just another one of his business consultations.

"Really?" said Kara. "Do any of *you* know how to perform the surgery?"

Jordan pulled back the last of Peter's restraints – really the last one this time – and he swivelled around, sitting up on the edge of the bed.

"Thanks," he said.

125

And before any of us realized what was happening, he tore across the room, smashing straight into Kara's chest and knocking her to the ground, out of Dad's hands.

"Peter, no!" Jordan shouted.

But the first punch had already landed on Kara's jaw.

Chapter 15

**Tuesday 30 June
44 days**

It was Mr Hanger all over again. Dad reached down to pull Peter off, but Peter grabbed Kara's hair, dragging her up with him. She screamed and Dad let go. Peter crashed down again, landing on top of Kara and driving her head into the lino.

"I'll – kill – you!" he grunted, hands shifting to her neck. "I'll – kill – you!"

A buzzing, crackling sound filled the room.

The lights started dimming on and off, like they'd done before.

"The pen!" Kara spluttered. "Jordan – please—!"

Peter took one hand back from Kara's neck and

mashed it down into her face, clawing at her eyes and mouth. She screamed again, twisting under him.

"*What pen?*" said Jordan frantically.

"The silver thing!" I shouted. "The sedative! Where is it?"

"No!" Peter yelled. "Don't – *don't you dare!*"

Dad wrapped his arms around Peter's middle. Peter struggled and shouted, but Dad had a better grip this time. He dragged Peter upright, away from Kara. She stared up at him, chest heaving. Blood oozed from the claw marks on her face.

"Behind you!" said Jordan. "The bench!"

I turned and grabbed it.

The lights dimmed again. There was a clatter of metal and the other bed suddenly flew across the room, away from Peter and Dad. It crashed into the wall and fell on its side.

"Luke – quickly!" said Dad, barely holding him.

"NO!" Peter flung a kick at my stomach.

I ducked out of the way and aimed the pen at his thigh. Peter wrenched his body around to look at me. "If you do this – If you—"

"I'm sorry," I said.

I drove the needle down into his leg.

"You *bastard!*" he screamed, convulsing like he

128

was being electrocuted. "*You stupid – freaking—!*"

"Peter, please," said Jordan. "We're not – We're on your side here."

"She wants us *dead!*" said Peter. He was still fighting, but I could tell that the sedative was getting to work.

Jordan took another step toward him, as close as she could get without being kicked.

"I know," she said, in a voice like she was saying goodbye to a dying person. "I know she does. But it's under control now, OK? Just – just try to be calm."

Peter's legs gave way and he sank down in Dad's arms. He gazed up at Jordan, a mess of hurt and fear.

I watched his eyes drift shut. My stomach felt like it was turning in on itself.

Dad hoisted Peter off the ground and laid him down on the bed. "This is the kid we came down here to rescue?"

"He's *sick*," I said, lowering Soren's head down on to the pillow. "He's not – something's happened to him."

Kara got up, bringing a hand to her bloodied jaw, making sure everything was still where it was supposed to be.

"How long will he be out for?" asked Jordan. She

was at the end of Peter's bed, picking up one of the papers he'd sent flying when he went to maul Kara.

Kara's eyes narrowed. "Why?"

"Answer the question," said Jordan.

Kara waited just long enough to let us think she wasn't going to answer. "Half an hour at most. The pens carry a single dose, and you already delivered most of *that* to my son. Peter only got whatever was left."

"Good." Jordan sat up on Peter's bed, eyes running down the page in her hand. "What's the time?"

Dad checked his watch. "Just after eleven."

"OK," said Jordan, mostly to herself. "OK, this can work."

I cringed. *What now?*

"All right, Overseer," said Jordan, looking up, "let me explain the situation to you. In less than an hour, Calvin's new security system is going online all over Phoenix. We need a new place to stay, which means you just got yourselves some new houseguests."

I watched for Kara's response. She stayed silent, but it looked like an effort.

"We also need you to get over thinking that all of this is our fault," Jordan went on. "Because I can't afford to be sleeping with one eye open every night.

So we're going to need to take Peter up to the surface and get him to show us—"

"*No,*" said Kara. "How can you even *think* of taking him up there? He's completely unstable!"

And as much as I hated to admit it, I kind of agreed with her.

"Jordan—" I began.

"We don't have a choice!" said Jordan. "Unless you know where he's got all our Tabitha stuff."

"All our Tabitha stuff" was the recording Bill had given us of Shackleton and Calvin discussing the end of the world, and a DVD of two Phoenix construction workers getting dismembered in a testing facility. Both had ended up somewhere in Peter's house.

Jordan was right. Peter would've made sure those recordings were well hidden. Taking him with us was the only way to make sure we found them in time.

"What about the security officers?" I said. "They'll still be at the house until—"

"Yeah, but look at this," said Jordan, handing me the page in her hand.

It was a blurry, zoomed-in, black and white image that looked like it had been captured from one of the original surveillance cameras in the security centre. It showed a big grid with *BURKE*, *HUNTER*, and *WEIR*

131

at the top, and a bunch of guards" names underneath, all designated either *INTERIOR* or *EXTERIOR*. A duty roster for all the officers guarding our houses.

Jordan pointed to the bottom of the *WEIR* column.

01/07 – 4 p.m. to 12 a.m.
COOK (INTERIOR)
MILLER (EXTERIOR)

Officer Miller. The guard who'd jumped on Calvin back at the crater, to give us a chance to get away. If we could get to him before the other guard saw us...

I sighed, handing back the paper.

"Great," said Jordan, apparently taking that as an agreement. She hopped down from the bed. "Well, I guess we'd better get going, then."

I looked down at Peter's unconscious body. "But—"

"The cameras go on at midnight," said Jordan, ignoring the explosive look on Kara's face. She turned to me. "So are you going to carry him, or are you going to make me do it?"

Chapter 16

Tuesday 30 June
44 days

"I don't get it," I said, trudging through the dark bush yet again, Peter's dead weight crushing into my shoulder. "Why is Miller even on that roster? Calvin knows he can't trust him."

"Calvin probably doesn't have a choice," said Jordan. "*He* might have decided to start killing everyone who gets in his way, but that doesn't mean Shackleton has. It would look pretty suss if Calvin just pulled Miller off duty for no reason. And I get the feeling Calvin's guys are pretty thin on the ground. For now, at least."

We were almost there. It had been a nightmare

getting Peter up those stairs but, once we were above ground, it was only a short walk to the edge of town.

Dad had stayed behind to keep an eye on Kara. I didn't like leaving him down there, but I knew it made sense. Besides, if he could dodge Shackleton's hitmen and sneak into Phoenix without getting killed, surely he could handle a middle-aged woman and her unconscious son. Unless one of them turned out to have some crazy superpower or whatever.

I used my mouth to pull back the sleeve from my free hand, and nudged the backlight button on Dad's watch with my nose.

11.18 p.m. Forty minutes to go.

I stepped sideways to avoid a rock and almost smashed into a tree as Peter suddenly started kicking his legs.

"Wha–?" he grunted. "Who – *hey!* Put me down! Let go of me, you freaking—!"

"*Shh!*" said Jordan, grabbing his face with both hands. "*Quiet!*"

I let him down before he knocked us both over. He straightened up and grabbed me by the front of my jumper. "What the crap do you reckon you're—?"

"Peter!" said Jordan. "Shut. *Up.*"

"Jordan..." He spun around and pulled her into a hug.

She pushed him away. "Yeah. Not now. Listen, we're on our way to your parents" house. We need to get the Tabitha DVD to show Kara and Soren."

"No," said Peter, threatening to flare up again. "Why? What are you doing, working with them?"

"We're not working with—"

"Yeah? Then why did *he* stick me with that bloody needle?" He jabbed a finger in my direction.

"Why do you think?" I said, even less sympathetic now that he was threatening to bash me.

"She sent Mike in to kidnap me! He abducted me from a freaking hospital bed!"

"And that means you get to beat her to a pulp, does it?" Jordan demanded.

Peter gave her one of those looks that said he was only backing down because it was her. "I – I didn't plan that. I don't know what happened."

"Look," said Jordan. "I'm sorry we left you and I'm sorry we didn't come back sooner. But things have changed. We can't go home anymore. We need to show Kara and Soren what's really going on up here because down *there* is the only safe place we've got left."

Peter took a minute to let all that sink in. I watched him, bracing myself in case he decided to blow up again.

"But – hang on. If we can't go home, then why are we walking back to my—?" He gave up, shoulders slumping. "Whatever. Let's go."

A couple of minutes later, we were peering out at Peter's house. Jordan had filled him in on the rest of what was going on, but that didn't stop him swearing under his breath when he saw the security officer standing in the shadows of his front porch.

"Is it Miller?" I asked, leaning forward through the bushes.

"Better be," said Jordan. She jumped up and dashed across the bike path.

"At least *some* things don't change," Peter muttered, as he and I scrambled after her.

The guard on the porch stiffened as we approached. He drew his gun.

My mind screamed, but my legs just kept hammering forward. Up to the house.

The guard jumped down the steps to meet us, weapon raised.

"Officer Miller!" Jordan breathed.

Miller reeled back.

"Get *out!*" he hissed, glancing back at the house. "Go! If anyone sees—"

"Yeah, yeah, we know," said Jordan. "But we have

to get in there. We need you to get the other guard away. Just for a few minutes."

"No. I can't."

"Please!" I checked the windows. Lights all off, but Officer Cook could be staring down from any of them. "Please, this is really important."

"He'll kill me," said Miller. "If Calvin finds out…"

"He *won't*," said Jordan. "He'll never know."

Miller lowered his gun. His collar shifted and I glimpsed the edge of a bandage marking the place where one of the other guards had shot him.

His face twisted uncomfortably.

"All right," he said. "Hurry up and get hidden."

"Thanks," Jordan whispered as he raced inside.

"Over here!" said Peter, leading us around the side of the house. I ducked down in the grass, chest still thundering like there was something trapped inside it.

I glanced up at the windowsill above our heads. What if Officer Cook had already seen us? I pictured him right there, right above us, slowly taking aim to splatter us against the side of the house.

The screen door crashed open and I stifled a shout.

"Quiet!" hissed Miller from back around the corner. "You want to wake his parents?"

"Where is he?" said Cook. He strode into view,

halfway up the front path.

"That way," said Miller, right behind him. "He ran when he saw me."

"He *ran?* I thought he was—"

And then they were out of earshot. The two guards bolted through the gate and up the street.

Jordan slipped around to the front of the house.

"This doesn't mean you're not insane," said Peter, slinking behind her. "Just because that worked…"

"Shh!" said Jordan.

I followed them in through the open door, checking the time again. 11.29 p.m. Half an hour.

Peter led the way upstairs. He reached his bedroom door, ignored it, and darted left. Heading for his parents" room.

My stomach turned. "Peter…"

The door opened just as he reached it.

Peter's dad rolled out in his wheelchair, teeth gritted. He was dressed in boxers and an old T-shirt, looking even more drawn and dishevelled than the last time I'd seen him. Between losing his legs and losing his son, it was like the last month had aged him about ten years.

"Dad!" said Peter, diving down to hug him.

"Wha— *Pete!*" he said. "Jess, get out here!"

"Mr Weir," I hissed, putting a finger to my lips.

Peter's dad looked up, eyes darkening again. "Where are the guards?"

"They're gone. But not for long," said Jordan. She put a hand on Peter's shoulder. "Where is it?"

"The windmill picture," said Peter, staring at his dad. "The one with Bill's note on the back. The DVDs are stuck under the frame."

"Right." She disappeared into his bedroom.

"Peter, where have you—?" Mr Weir paused, finally releasing his son. "Wait. You're walking! I thought Shackleton—"

"Yeah, he did," said Peter, straightening up to hug his mum as she appeared in the doorway, dressed in a nightgown. "But the people who took me—"

"Peter," I said, glancing down the stairs. "We don't really have time for this."

Peter pulled away from his mum and I took a step back in case he decided to attack me again. But then he nodded. "Yeah. I'll explain later. We need to get you out of here before the guards come back."

There was a smashing sound and a tinkling of broken glass from the next room. Jordan obviously wasn't wasting any time getting that picture frame undone.

"Peter, slow down," said Mrs Weir, resting her hands on Mr Weir's shoulders. "What *is* all this? Why are they after you?"

"Because they're trying to kill everyone outside of Phoenix," said Peter, "and we're trying to stop them."

His parents stared. Peter glanced nervously between them. The silence stretched out.

Finally, Peter's mum closed her eyes. "OK," she said in a hollow voice. "So … what do we need to do?"

I felt a twinge of jealousy. One sentence and she was right on board. Meanwhile, my mum was shacking up with Dr Frankenstein.

I pushed the feeling aside. It wasn't their fault my mum was a moron.

Jordan came up behind me. "Time to go," she said, touching my arm.

I nodded at Peter's mum and dad. "They're coming too."

Jordan glanced at Mr Weir's wheelchair for a second. "All right. But someone's going to need to—"

"No," said Mr Weir. "We're staying."

"*What?*" Peter dropped down, eye to eye with his dad. "No freaking way. You can't. Don't you get what's going on?"

Mr Weir rapped the side of his wheelchair. "Yeah, mate. I get it."

"They can fix you!" said Peter. "There's a doctor down there."

"Down where?" his mum asked.

"No, don't," said Peter's dad. "It's safer if we don't know. Just as long as – you'll be out of sight of the new security system, right?"

"*Yes,*" said Peter, "which is exactly why we need to hurry up and get you *out* of here!"

But I'd suddenly realized where Mr Weir was coming from. "We can't," I said.

Peter's head snapped up at me. "We bloody well *can!*"

"No, Peter – the suppressor," I said. "They're still tracking him."

"We'd have to be quick," said Jordan. "Straight out and into the bush before—"

"Then what?" said Mr Weir, shaking his head. "Say we make it back to wherever you kids are hiding – how do we deal with Shackleton if we can't set foot inside the town?"

"Hold on," said Jordan slowly. "You're saying you *want* to stay here? You want to keep working with us from the inside."

"What do you mean *keep* working?" asked Peter, standing up.

"He distracted Shackleton for us," I said. "The night we found you. He was the one who—"

"You used *him?*" said Peter, fists balling up. "After what Shackleton did to Reeve, you thought you'd just send my dad in to follow in his bloody footsteps?"

"Calm down, Pete." Mr Weir reached for Peter's hand. "They didn't *use* me. I wanted the job. And now you're back, so I reckon I must've done all right."

Peter's hands relaxed a bit. He kept glaring at me, but didn't say anything.

"Pete, look at me," said Mr Weir, pulling Peter back down to eye level. "I understand how dangerous this is. But you can't take on Shackleton by yourself. And we're your *parents*. It's about bloody time you let us step in here."

Peter looked up at his mum, a tortured expression on his face.

She shivered, pulling her dressing gown tighter around herself. "All right, let me preface this by saying I have no idea what any of you are talking about. But if Dad thinks us staying here is going to be best for you … then that's what we'll do."

Peter slowly stretched to his feet and hugged her

again. "How the crap am I letting you do this?"

"Because you know it's the right thing," said Mr Weir.

Peter let go of his mum. "Better be."

"We've got access to the security feeds around town," I said, turning toward the stairs. I didn't want to pull the family apart again, but we'd been here too long already. "If you need to get our attention, just get in front of one of the old cameras."

"Also," said Jordan to Mrs Weir, "if you happened to be riding up that bike path over the road and *accidentally* dropped a newspaper into—"

A crash from downstairs ended our conversation. The screen door flying open again.

The security guards were back inside.

Chapter 17

"Quick!" said Mr Weir, jabbing a finger at his bedroom door. "Hide. I'll get rid of them."

But it was already too late for that.

The light over the stairs flashed on. Cook was walking up, weapon raised. Miller raced up behind him, drawing his own gun, playing along.

At least, I hoped that was all he was doing.

"All of you, stay right where you are!" said Cook. "First one to move gets a bullet."

Officer Cook's hands were shaking. He reminded me of Mike. In too deep and overcompensating by getting all trigger-happy.

"Come on, mate," said Peter, raising his hands above his head. He stepped across to the top of the stairs, looking not quite himself. "You don't want to—"

"I said *don't move*," Cook snapped, still edging closer.

Peter leant toward him as he approached. I had just enough time to be surprised at his sudden rush of courage before—

BLAM!

He leapt at Cook.

There was a smash of glass and the house went dark again as Cook's bullet shot through the light fixture above our heads. Mrs Weir screamed.

Peter and Cook went rolling over each other down the stairs, almost taking Miller with them as they tumbled past.

"Pete!" yelled Mr Weir, as Jordan and I bolted down.

Below us, Peter and Cook had already hit the bottom. Cook's gun was gone, but he was getting up on his hands and knees, pinning Peter to the ground by the shoulders.

Jordan leapt down the last few stairs. I dashed after her, reaching the ground just in time to hear

Peter let out a strangled roar.

And then, impossibly, Cook was flying backwards.

SMASH!

He went straight through the front window, on to the verandah on the other side, one of his legs still hooked over the windowsill.

I stared down at Peter, who was flat on his back in the hall. "What was *that?*"

He got to his feet, grimacing, right hand clutching his shoulder, and ran for the front door.

"Wait – stop!" called Officer Miller, thundering down behind us.

Jordan dashed after Peter.

What just happened?

It was impossible.

But what did that even mean anymore?

"Luke!" Mr Weir called down. "What's going on?"

Hard to say, I thought, heading outside.

"Stay there!" I called back over my shoulder.

Mr Weir started grumbling that he didn't have much choice, but by then I was out the door.

Cook was on his feet again, backed up against the bike rack at the far end of the verandah. Even in the dull glow of the porch light, I could tell that he was

146

bleeding pretty badly.

Peter stepped toward him, maniac fire in his eyes.

"Miller!" Cook roared. "Get out here!"

Officer Miller stepped into the doorway.

"Peter, come on," I said. "Time to go."

I grabbed his arm to pull him away. He jumped at the touch and spun around, sending a fist rocketing toward my face. I don't know if he even knew it was me. I reeled out of the way, knocking into Jordan, finding my feet just in time to stop both of us falling down the verandah steps.

Officer Cook took advantage of the distraction. He ran at Peter, grabbing him around the middle. They wrestled to the ground again and somehow Peter got back on top. He grabbed the officer's wrists, squeezing like he was trying to snap them right off.

"Peter!" I yelled. "*Leave* him!"

Miller pushed past me, into the fray. I stepped aside, and caught something moving in my peripheral vision. *Oh, great.* Two more officers were coming up the street.

I doubled back. "Jordan!"

She was up the other end of the verandah, and—

No. Oh no. Not now.

Jordan was bent double over the railing, coughing

and shuddering, fighting for breath. Halfway into another one of her visions.

I moved to help her, one eye still locked on the approaching guards. "Jordan!"

She stopped shaking.

"Hey. You OK?" I asked. "Are you here?"

Her eyes opened and she took in a gasping breath.

I backed off a bit. "Jordan...?"

She got up from the railing, slipped past me, and started down the steps.

"No – wait!" I said.

No response. The two guards bolted in through the front gate, but Jordan just kept walking like she couldn't see them. Which, obviously, she couldn't.

I gave Peter one last backward glance before going after Jordan. Miller had got well and truly dragged into it now, and it was kind of hard to tell who was fighting who.

One insane disaster at a time. Was that really so much to ask?

Jordan was still headed straight for the guards.

"Hey – hold it!" said the guy in front. Blonde hair. Glasses glinting in the darkness. Only a few years older than me. I'd seen him before, but back then he'd been working a coffee cart outside the mall.

One of Calvin's new recruits, I realized.

He raised his gun at Jordan and all thoughts flew from my mind.

"Put it down!" said the other guard, an older guy I didn't recognize. "If you shoot her, Shackleton'll—"

SMASH!

The guards" eyes shot to the verandah.

A whole section of the railing had just blasted apart. Officer Cook sailed out on to the lawn, crashing to the grass in the middle of a pile of broken wood palings.

Peter stood silhouetted on the verandah, staring down at the crumpled guard.

I couldn't see Miller anywhere.

"Hey!" shouted Coffee Cart Guard again. "Hey! I told you to *stop.*"

Jordan was seconds from slamming straight into them. The older guard reached out to grab her. His hands closed in on her shoulders—

And they kept going. Straight *through* her body.

"Aahh!" I shouted, jolting back.

The guard gasped and jumped aside, staring down at his hands like they were infected with something.

I heard screams from over the fence. Neighbours, coming out to watch.

Coffee Cart Guard backed up, raising his gun again, point-blank at Jordan's chest.

"STOP!" I ran forward. "You can't—!"

BLAM!

I ducked down, hands over my head. "NO!"

More screaming.

I opened my eyes again. Jordan was still walking. Unharmed, unflinching. The bullet had gone right through her, like she wasn't even there.

Jordan closed in on Coffee Cart Guard. He dived out of her way, dropping his gun. She gazed off to her left, eyes widening in shock at something none of us could see.

Someone shot past me, a shadow charging across the grass. Peter, running at Coffee Cart Guard, low growls rumbling in his throat. He'd seen him fire on Jordan, and he was not happy.

Coffee Cart Guard jumped to his feet, fumbling with his gun, and then—

I don't know what happened.

Suddenly he was shooting across the lawn like a soccer ball. Peter hadn't even *touched* him. The guard crashed into the front fence and landed in a heap. Peter ran after him.

I felt like my head was caving in. Too much

insanity all at once. I mean, obviously Phoenix had never been *normal*, but I thought we were all still obeying the laws of physics, at least.

Jordan was running now. She stopped at the fence and reached down, pulling frantically at the empty air, like the gate wasn't open already.

"Jordan!" I shouted, closing the gap between us.

I grabbed her shoulder, or *tried* to anyway. My hand went straight through her. She ran out on to the street, oblivious.

I surged forward, grabbing at her again, and this time my hand made contact. "Jordan! Come on—!"

"No!" she moaned.

"Jordan!" I dragged her around to face me. "Jordan! Get back here!"

She started shaking again. Gagging with her whole body. I clutched her arms, holding her at a distance in case she decided to vomit on me. I checked the street. No more security yet, but plenty of freaked-out neighbours.

My hands slipped on Jordan's arms, like for a second she was fading away again. "No! No, come on – seriously Jordan, if you don't—"

Jordan's body jolted one last time and she gasped. *"Luke!"*

She was back.

"We need to go," I said. "Peter's—"

A startled shout cut through the chaos in Peter's yard. The last guard standing was no longer standing. He *bounced* across the grass, a human tumbleweed, hurtling away from Peter, until he smacked into the side of the house.

More sounds of horror from the neighbours.

"Was that—?" said Jordan, mouth falling open. "Did *he* do that?"

Peter straightened up, swaying unsteadily. He stared at the crumpled figure across the yard, then turned toward us and clambered over the fence. His steps were slow and uneven, like he'd worn himself out too much to even walk straight.

"Hurry!" I hissed. Half the lights in the street were on by now. People were keeping their distance, but they were watching.

I couldn't wait to see what Shackleton came up with to make this one go away.

Peter lurched closer. As he moved out into the streetlight, I saw blood glistening on his fists, and more trickling down from his nose.

Jordan took his arm, pulling him toward the bush.

"Did you see me?" Peter swayed again, flashing

her a sickening smile. "I did it. I – I saved you." He pitched forward and slumped to the ground.

Unconscious. Again.

"Are you *serious?*" I muttered.

I wrapped my arms around his waist and got him up over my shoulder, my legs buckling under his weight.

"You got him?" said Jordan, sweeping the crowd in case anyone decided to try something.

"Yeah," I grunted, and took one last look at the house. I could see the dark shapes of Peter's parents watching from their bedroom window.

I turned away and followed Jordan into the bush.

Chapter 18

The tunnel entrance rolled open.

I looked around, making sure we weren't being watched. But I guess Peter's neighbours had seen enough of his rampage to put them off following us.

Jordan slipped into the ground as soon as the gap was wide enough. I staggered after her, nearly losing Peter for a second, and scratched around for the button on the wall. But someone downstairs was already taking care of it. As soon as my head dropped clear, the entrance started rumbling shut again.

Down was definitely easier than up, but it was still slow going with Peter on my back. More than once, his weight shifted unexpectedly and the two of us almost went sailing over the edge of the stairs.

"Someone should really let these guys know about the invention of the lift," I grumbled as we finally reached the bottom, breaking the silence for the first time since we'd left Peter's place.

Jordan turned to look at me, and I stopped short at the expression on her face. She looked pale. Sick. Eyes clouded over with a scarily un-Jordan-like dread. I could tell right away that it was about more than what we'd just seen up on the surface.

More than what *I'd* just seen up there, anyway.

Dad came running up the hallway toward us. Kara trailed after him.

"Is everyone OK?" Dad asked. He frowned at Peter, then reached out to pull him down from my shoulders. "He didn't wake up?"

Kara scoffed, snatching up one of Peter's bloodied hands. "He didn't do *this* in his sleep." She shot a nasty look at Jordan and me. "If only someone had warned you about taking him up to the surface."

Jordan pulled two discs from the pocket of her jumper. Kara snatched them out of her hand.

"He was— He's worse than before," I said, as Dad hoisted Peter up into his arms. I stared at the trickle of

155

dried blood streaking down over Peter's mouth.

"Of course he's worse than before," Kara muttered.

She was halfway up the corridor before I realized what she'd just said.

"Hey, what?" I said, racing to catch up. "You *know* what's happening to him?"

Kara pushed into the lab and picked up an auto-injector pen. She snapped it open and tipped out a little plastic cartridge. "He's deteriorating," she said, pulling a new cartridge from a box on the bench.

Jordan appeared in the doorway. "What's that supposed to mean?"

"It means he needs to be dealt with," Kara loaded the new cartridge into the pen and clicked it shut, "before the situation becomes *truly* unpleasant."

She jabbed Peter's leg as soon as Dad brought him through the door.

"Not unconscious enough already?" said Dad.

Kara pocketed the pen and took the discs across to the surveillance room. Dad laid Peter down and we followed her through.

Kara cursed under her breath as she entered the room.

My eyes dropped to the circle of laptops and I saw why. The security feeds were gone, replaced by the same error message on every screen.

Connection lost.

I glanced down at my watch. 12.04 a.m.

The new security system was online. And it looked like the old one had been made redundant.

Kara sat at one of the computers and dismissed the error message, sticking the first disc into the drive. A window popped up with a single audio file.

"Crazy Bill gave this to us the week I got here," I told Dad.

Dad raised an eyebrow. "You're getting your information from someone called *Crazy*—?"

"Do you want me to hear this or not?" said Kara, turning to glare at us.

She opened the file. And even though we must've listened to this conversation a hundred times by now, I still held my breath like I was hearing it for the first time.

"I take it our final arrivals have landed?" asked a casual voice, over the static.

"Yes, sir," replied a second voice. *"Aaron is showing them to their living quarters as we speak."*

"Nothing concerning to report?"

Kara spun around on her chair again. "Who are these people?"

"Seriously?" I said. "That's Shackleton and Calvin. They're the people *running* this place!"

"*No, sir. The boy has a father on the outside with whom he was quite fixated on getting in touch,*" said Calvin.

Dad squeezed my shoulder. He was smiling, almost triumphant, and for the first time in forever I felt like maybe we'd actually achieved something. It was just one more person against the whole of the Co-operative, but it was *something*.

The conversation continued, and Dad's smile vanished. We'd already told him most of what was in the recording, but that wasn't the same as hearing it for himself. There's a difference between a set of facts in your head and actually *knowing* something.

"*In a hundred days, there won't* be *anyone left on the outside!*" said Shackleton, losing patience. "*Until that time, it is imperative that the people of Phoenix remain under the belief that their lives are progressing as normal.*"

Kara was a statue. The colour had drained away from her skin and she was gripping the second disc so hard I thought it was going to snap, but the fierce, stony expression on her face hadn't shifted a millimetre.

"A hundred days, Bruce," said Shackleton, bringing the conversation to a close. *"That's all. A hundred more days and then this will all be over."*

Dad's arm came down around my shoulder again. He looked at me like he had something important to say, but couldn't get the words out.

"You're alive," he managed eventually.

I breathed out. "Yeah."

And I guess that was an achievement too.

Kara ejected the first disc and slotted in the second. In a minute, she'd be watching a couple of Co-operative employees get torn to shreds in slow motion.

Jordan hovered in the doorway. The same despair was still etched across her face, like she'd just been told she was dying.

"Come on," I whispered, as a creepy-looking brown-haired woman appeared on the screen. "We don't need to watch this again."

I pulled her back out into the lab. She turned to face me and my hands reached automatically for hers. "What did you see?" I asked.

Jordan tilted her head, obviously surprised that I'd guessed what she was thinking about. Like it wasn't all over her face. She swallowed. "They were taking my family."

"Calvin?" I said.

"Yeah," said Jordan. "Well, two of his men. They had Mum and Georgia, at least. I don't know about Dad. Georgia was—" She rolled her head back, trying to stop the tears. "She was *screaming*, and they were just—"

"When?" I asked.

"I don't know. Morning."

Jordan bit her lip, thinking. "It was a Saturday," she said. "Georgia was in her soccer stuff. But she wears her uniform to bed on Friday nights, so it could've been—"

"Why does she do that?" I asked.

"Because she's six!" said Jordan, exasperated. "How should I know?"

"OK," I said, searching for some way to be reassuring. "OK, so—"

Dad came out to join us and my mind went blank. He sat back against one of the benches, slowly shaking his head.

Kara walked out after him, arms folded. I'd expected her to look disturbed, and she did, but there was something else in her expression too. Cold calculation. Like she still knew something we didn't and was trying to quickly add it all up.

But Jordan was clearly in no mood to string this out. "Well?" she snapped.

"Yes," said Kara, exasperated. "You may stay here. For the time being. You're hardly giving me a choice, are you?" Not a hint of apology for everything she'd put us through.

"Thanks," said Jordan, rolling her eyes. She strode across the room and grabbed Kara by the front of her coat. "Now, how about filling us in on exactly *why* you've been watching us all this time?"

Kara glanced down at Jordan's hands. She raised an eyebrow. "And why would I want to do that?"

"Are you kidding?" I said. "How about the part where you abducted Peter and held us all prisoner down here? You don't think you owe us a few answers after that?"

But if I'd been expecting those recordings of ours to magically transform Kara from enemy to ally, I was way off the mark.

She detached herself from Jordan. "I don't owe you any such thing. I am offering you sanctuary while we resolve this situation. But I am a long way from offering you my trust."

"No, of course not," spat Jordan. "We've only risked our lives to bring you proof of who's really behind this. Why should that be any reason to trust us?"

Kara faltered for just a second, like maybe she was going to hear Jordan out, but then she pushed on again. "As I said, this is at best a temporary measure. And for as long as you are guests in my home—"

"Fine. Whatever." Jordan nodded in the direction of the hallway. "C'mon Luke, let's go."

"What?" said Kara and I at the same time.

Jordan was already halfway across the room. "We're going back for my family."

"Now?" I said. "No. We can't. Even if those cameras *hadn't* just – you're only a few blocks up the road from Peter's place. We wouldn't even get close."

"We have to!" said Jordan. "My mum's about to be—"

"And my mum is up there playing happy families with Montag," I cut in. "But we can't just—"

Dad looked up. "Sorry?"

Ugh, I thought. Not exactly how I'd planned on letting that news come out.

"Saturday, right?" I pushed on, catching her in the doorway. "That's when Calvin's coming for them?"

"Yeah, probably, but—"

"So we've got some time," I said. "Three days to

figure out a way in."

"And what if we can't?" said Jordan.

"Then we can still go running blindly into the path of danger. But not tonight. Jordan – we can't just keep going like this. We need to *sleep*."

As soon as the words were out of my mouth, I realized just how tired I was. Tonight had been nuts, even by our standards, and neither of us had had a full night's sleep since we'd left home a week ago.

Jordan sighed. She pulled me in, wrapping her arms around my back, forehead resting on my shoulder. "Sorry," she said. "This is all just so…"

"I know it is," I said stupidly, hugging her back, suddenly very aware of Dad and Kara. "We'll figure it out in the morning."

"There's another room across the hall," said Dad, letting the Montag comment slide for the moment. "A living area. There's a beanbag and a couple of couches." He stood up from the bench and looked to Kara. "Do you have any spare blankets?"

Kara pursed her lips, reminding me uncomfortably of Mum. "I'll see what I can find."

"What about Peter?" Jordan asked, stepping away from me.

"He'll need to be strapped down again," said Kara.

"For his own safety as much as anyone's," she added, at the look on Jordan's face. "I'll find a more long-term solution tomorrow."

Jordan and I looked at each other. I shrugged and nodded. I didn't like it, but after tonight, it didn't seem like an argument we could win.

Kara walked out of the room, and Dad followed.

Jordan and I went over to Peter's bed. Jordan straightened out his legs and we started fastening his straps again.

I spotted a box of tissues on the bench next to me. I ran one under some water and wiped the blood away from Peter's face, trying not to think about how much worse things were probably going to get when he woke up.

Chapter 19

"But she heard it herself!" said Jordan angrily. "She *heard* Shackleton planning it all. What more proof does she need that we're not the ones they should be fighting?"

I watched her scrape the last few dregs of porridge from the bottom of her bowl. We'd only been up for an hour or so, but I'd already lost count of how many times we'd circled around to that question.

"Maybe she thinks we're working *with* Shackleton," I said.

"Right," said Jordan. "That would be why he keeps trying to kill us."

We were sitting on one of the springy old couches in the living area where we'd spent the night. We hadn't seen Kara or Soren yet that morning, but there was a little kitchen at the other end of the room, and we'd helped ourselves to some breakfast.

Dad was over on the beanbag, making up for lost sleep. We'd decided to take turns keeping watch through the night, just in case. Dad had volunteered for the first shift, and I'd woken up ten hours later to find him still sitting there, watching the door.

"I think maybe proof isn't the problem," I said. "Because, yeah, it's not like we haven't given her enough of that to go on. But I think maybe it's not about that. I think this is about whatever made her decide to go after us in the first place. She still trusts that more than she trusts us."

"She's a moron," said Jordan, dropping her bowl on to the carpet.

I was pretty sure it wasn't that simple. But considering last night's vision of her family getting dragged off by security, it wasn't surprising that Jordan seemed a bit less calm and rational than usual.

The door opened and Kara walked in, shooting a disapproving look at the bowls on the floor. "Come with me."

"Come with you where?" asked Jordan, getting up.

Kara turned back toward the door. "There's something I need to show you."

I looked down at Dad and wondered if we should wake him.

"Let him sleep," said Kara. "We're not going to do anything to him."

"Where's Soren?" I asked.

"He's working," said Kara.

She took us down the grimy corridor that led into the mess of half-destroyed rooms where they'd first held us prisoner. There were lights on now, and it was easier to see what it all might have looked like, back when it was up and running.

"What was this all for?" I asked, glancing through a gap in the wall at what looked like a huge microscope, half-drowned in the concrete. "What were you guys doing down here?"

"Research," said Kara, in a tone that said that was all the answer I was going to get.

Again, I was forcibly reminded of Mum. The more I talked to Kara, the more I thought the two of them could have been best friends in another life.

"You worked for Remi Vattel, right?" said Jordan.

"She was the one who—"

"I didn't *work* for Remi Vattel," said Kara irritably. "She was my mother."

The corridor opened up in front of us and I spotted a familiar leather couch to our right. We were back at the room where they'd tied me up.

Kara stopped at the door. They'd riveted a metal plate across the little window, shrinking the gap so it was barely big enough to fit a hand through. Underneath, three thick steel bars stretched out across the door on metal brackets, barricading it shut.

"This is where we'll be holding Peter," said Kara.

Jordan clenched her teeth. "What?"

I could already tell this was going to be a short conversation. I had maybe thirty seconds until it degenerated into a brawl.

"We'll keep him sedated as much as possible, of course," said Kara, "however—"

"No we *won't*," said Jordan. "You think you get to make that decision?"

Kara's eyes glinted behind her glasses. "Would you like to present an alternative?"

"He's not an animal!" Jordan shouted. "You can't just lock him up and—"

"Jordan..." I braced myself, knowing this would

probably get me ripped to bits.

She took a step away from me. "No. Luke, you can't be OK with this!"

"I'm not," I said, in what I hoped was a calming voice. I turned to Kara. "You're not sedating him. He stays awake. And Jordan and I get to come in and see him whenever we want."

"Luke—" Jordan tried again.

"You get him a bed," I went on, wanting to get this all out before the argument had a chance to escalate. "And food, and clothes. And books to read, and – whatever he wants. And we figure out a way for him to wash and go to the toilet in an actual bathroom."

Kara wouldn't like it. But with Dad here and us back on our feet again, the situation had changed, and she knew it. That's why she'd "let us stay" without any real fight. And why she was showing us Peter's cell instead of trying to put us back in our own.

"All right," she said. "Yes. Fine. I'll organise it."

My eyes drifted back to the barricaded door. A week ago, it had been me beaten up and lying on the ground in there. And now...

"So that's it, huh?" said Jordan. "He's just a prisoner?"

"What else are we supposed to do?" I asked.

"You saw what he did to those guards! Something's *happening* to him. This is the only way to—"

"What about me?" Jordan asked. "Am I getting locked up too?"

Kara shot her a piercing look.

"Jordan, no," I said, "that's not what's—"

"Mum!" echoed a voice from further down the corridor. Soren barrelled into the room with a safety helmet on his head and a pickaxe over his shoulder.

He barged straight past Jordan and me. "It's open. Come and look."

Kara nodded. Then, to me: "We're finished here. Why don't you head back and see if your father's up yet?"

Soren twitched, as though he'd just realized that we were there too.

"No," said Jordan. "No, I think we'll come with you."

Kara narrowed her eyes but didn't argue. The three of us followed Soren deeper into the ruined building. The further we went, the more the concrete pressed in around us. I watched the pickaxe swaying on Soren's shoulder – it wasn't the first time we'd seen one of them lugging it around – and it finally dawned on me what they were doing with it.

"You've been, like, excavating this place, haven't

you?" I said. "Digging it all up out of the concrete."

No answer.

We reached a particularly narrow section of the pathway, and I had to turn sideways just to fit through. I squeezed out the other side and sped up to reach Jordan. "I'm sorry," I whispered. And then, when she didn't respond, "You think I don't hate this just as much as you do? But we can't just let him…"

"Run wild?" said Jordan.

"That's not—What else can we do? He isn't safe."

Jordan shook her head. "Soren's walking around with a pickaxe. You think that's safe?"

"Jordan—"

But Soren and Kara had just stopped up ahead. To our left was an even narrower tunnel that had been dug out of the concrete wall. We crawled through on our hands and knees.

"I assume this is all stable," Kara said.

"Yes," said Soren. "I've checked everything. Almost half the room is still intact."

By the end of the tunnel it was so dark we were making our way completely by touch. There was a thudding of feet up ahead – Soren dropping down from the other end – and a torch blinked on.

The rest of us piled out after him. Soren's tunnel

mustn't have been completely straight, because it was about a metre drop down into the room on the other side.

The air was mouldy and stale. It was like breaking into an old crypt or something.

Soren grabbed Jordan's hand to help her up. She shook him off.

Kara took the torch from Soren and shone it around. "Yes," she said, in a tone I couldn't figure out. "This is it."

But as far as I could tell, the room was completely empty. One and a half still-intact walls, and more of the same ragged concrete.

"What happens now?" asked Soren.

Kara didn't answer. Didn't seem to *have* an answer.

The torch beam fell to the floor and Jordan gasped. I followed her eyes and shuddered, realising what she'd seen.

Blood. Old and dried up, but definitely a blood stain. And *big*. Whoever this blood belonged to, they definitely hadn't left here alive.

"What is this place?" I breathed. "What happened here?"

Soren let out a harsh, breathy laugh. A sound like an animal. It echoed off the walls.

"Believe me," said Kara. "You don't want to know."

Chapter 20

Wednesday 1 July
43 days

I leant forward on the couch, arms on my knees, staring across at the barricaded door. Waiting for Peter to wake up. Jordan was next to me, but neither of us had spoken since we sat down.

We'd spent the rest of the morning setting up Peter's room, and moved him in there about an hour ago. The whole time, Jordan didn't say a word more than she had to.

I couldn't deal with it. I knew Peter would be mad at me, that was nothing new, but if I screwed things up with Jordan...

What hope did we have against the Co-operative

if *we* couldn't even stay on the same side?

All morning, I'd been looking for a way to fix things with Jordan. Looking for something I could say to put things back to normal. But what was there?

I knew part of it wasn't even about Peter. It was about her family being in danger. Until we could get them out, *everything* was going to be partly about that.

I closed my eyes.

Peter. Jordan's family. Kara and Soren. Mum. Mike, Cat and Tank. Jeremy's disappearance. Jordan's visions. The security cameras.

Tabitha.

It was already impossible. Already way beyond anything we could handle. If Jordan gave up on me—

I felt the couch shift, and suddenly her hand was resting on my knee. My eyes snapped open.

"Luke … I shouldn't—"

She sighed. I turned to face her properly, panic signals blaring inside my head.

Jordan bit her lip and tried again. "You did the right thing," she said. "I hate it, but it was right."

"Jordan—"

"No, just let me apologize, will you? You're right. He's not safe. I *know* he's not. But if this is what's happening to *him*—"

"That's him," I said firmly. "That's not you."

"Not yet," said Jordan.

I reached across to – to what? Hug her? But there was a smash of metal on concrete from across the room and we both looked up.

"What the crap is this?"

"Think he might be awake," said Jordan, getting to her feet.

Peter's eyes appeared behind the window, widening as we approached. "Hey! Get me out!"

"Shh!" said Jordan, meeting him at the door. "Calm down. It's OK." She started lifting the first metal barricade out of its brackets. Slowly, like she didn't want Peter to know what she was doing.

"What's going on?" Peter demanded.

"Hang on," I said, bending down to get the next barricade. "We're coming in."

"Screw that," said Peter. "I'm coming *out.*"

"You can't," said Jordan, and I was glad it was her saying it, and not me. "You need to – just hang on a sec, OK? We'll explain when we get inside."

I lifted the last metal bar from across the door. Jordan pulled it open just enough to slip through. I squeezed in after her, fingers brushing across a lump in my pocket. The auto-injector pen I'd taken from the lab, just in case.

The room inside might almost have passed for a bedroom, if not for the misshapen walls. We'd dragged in one of the dozen unused beds from the back of Soren's room, as well as a desk and a spare laptop that Kara had only given us after we'd threatened to change our minds about agreeing to keep Peter in here. Jordan had also scraped together a stack of old books and magazines on a little bookcase, and stolen the beanbag from the living area.

Still, there was no shaking the prison-cell vibe as we shut the door behind us.

"Are you OK?" asked Peter, reaching out to touch Jordan. "What's going on? How come I'm locked up if you're—?"

"Come and sit," said Jordan, pulling free and moving across to the bed.

Peter didn't need telling twice. There was more than enough room, but he sat down right next to her, leg pressing against hers, like he was *trying* to be creepy.

The metal chair – the one I'd been tied to, back when this was *my* prison – was lying on its side, kicked halfway across the room. I brought it over and sat opposite Peter and Jordan, the memory of the room still too close for comfort. I glanced at the arm of the chair and rubbed a bit of dried blood away with my thumb.

"Where are Kara and Soren?" Peter asked.

"They're back in the lab," said Jordan, shuffling away from him, but trying to make it subtle.

"What, strapped to the beds?"

My fingers traced back over the auto-injector. *Here it comes...*

"No..." said Jordan slowly. "They're – they're trying to get the surveillance room up and running again."

"My dad's keeping an eye on them," I added quickly.

Peter ignored me, attention still fixed on Jordan. "Then what the *crap* am I doing in here?"

"Peter, this isn't—" Jordan faltered, looking to me for support.

But what was I supposed to say that wasn't going to get me smashed in the face?

"It was Kara's decision," I said. "After you attacked her, and after what happened up on the surface..."

"*Kara's* decision?" said Peter angrily. "Why is freaking *Kara* deciding *anything?*"

"She's not. It's not like that."

"What about Shackleton? Is he on the panel too?

I mean, seeing as we're deciding things by bloody consensus now."

Jordan squirmed uncomfortably. "Peter…"

"No, screw this." Peter stood up.

My hand shot down to my pocket again.

Jordan caught the back of Peter's shirt. "Stop."

"Why?"

"What do you think Kara and Soren are going to do if you go out there?"

"They're going to get out of my freaking way," said Peter, pulling away from her.

I stood up, getting between him and the door, fingers curling around the auto-injector.

Peter snarled. "Get out of it, mate."

"Wait," I said, slowly drawing the pen out of my pocket. "Please, just stop—"

Peter's hand shot to my arm. He dragged it up into the air, digging his fingers in.

"Bastard," he growled, surging forward and punch-ing me in the gut. I grunted, dropped the pen and tried to back off, but he still had my other hand.

Peter slammed into me with his shoulder, shoving me toward the wall. I stumbled, feet dragging, hurtling backwards towards the mishmash of concrete and rust and nails.

"STOP!" Jordan screamed. "STOP IT!"

Peter pulled up, centimetres from driving me into a rusty pipe. He let go of me and whirled around.

"This is *exactly* why you're in here!" said Jordan. "Look at you! You're *sick*."

"No!" said Peter, holding up his hands. "No, I'm not, I was only—"

"What about those guards back at your house? How can we—?" Jordan's voice caught in her throat. "We don't even know if they're alive!"

"*You're* alive," said Peter, walking back to her.

I edged sideways, trying to stay out of his peripheral vision long enough to retrieve the pen.

"That's not the point!" said Jordan. "You can't just—"

"I had to," he whispered, moving to put his arms around her. "For you. I want us to be—"

She shuddered, twisting away, slipping out under his arm.

"No, wait!" said Peter, face falling.

I bent down and grabbed the auto-injector.

Jordan kept walking, straight out the door.

Peter started after her and I straightened up, ready to fend off another attack. He stopped, just out of arm's reach, seeing the pen in my hand.

179

He sighed heavily.

When he looked up again, there were tears running down his face.

Peter turned away, collapsing into the beanbag, head in his hands.

I shoved the pen back into my pocket and walked out of the room.

Chapter 21

"Still nothing?" said Kara, circling the table of laptops in the surveillance room.

"I'm trying," said Soren defensively. He'd been working all yesterday afternoon and most of today to access the new security system, but still the only image we had was from their own camera, up above the tunnel entrance.

Right now, that was the only one I cared about.

Jordan was up on the surface. She'd left about an hour ago to see if Peter's mum had dropped us off a newspaper or anything. I'd made her *promise* to stay away from town, but that didn't keep my brain from swimming with images of Calvin gunning her down on the front lawn of her house.

I hadn't spoken to Peter again since yesterday. Jordan had taken him some dinner last night, but he'd just thrown it back out through the hole in the door. She'd tried again at breakfast and come back pretending not to cry.

That was when she'd decided to take the trip outside.

Something moved across the screen. I was halfway out of my seat before I realized it was only a bird. I sank back down and kept watching.

Soren's fingers hammered away at a keyboard on the other side of the desk. Kara leant in behind him, resting her hands on the back of his chair. He twitched his head around. "Go away."

Kara backed off and left him to it.

"Still not back yet?" asked Dad, coming in from the other room.

"No," I sighed, spinning around on the chair. "I don't get what's taking – whoa."

Dad's raggedy Crazy Bill beard had disappeared. His hair was clean and combed, and he'd changed into some of Soren's spare clothes.

"What's wrong?" he asked, pulling up a chair next to me.

"Nothing," I said. "You just look like you again."

Dad glanced at the screen.

"So," he said, completely failing to sound offhand, "this Montag guy..."

Something tightened in my chest. But I knew I couldn't avoid this conversation forever. "Robert Montag. He's our doctor. *Their* doctor. The head of Phoenix Medical."

Dad gave a slow nod. "And he and Mum are...?"

"More than just good friends. Yeah."

Another nod, still determinedly casual. "What's he like?"

"*What's he like?*" I said. "Dad, he's one of them! He helped build this place."

Dad sat up in his chair, and this time I was sure he was going to lose it. But he just took a deep breath, rested his elbows back on the desk, and said, "I assume Mum doesn't know about that part."

"Only because she's too bloody stupid to hear it," I muttered, chest twisting even tighter.

"But you've tried," said Dad. He nodded wearily. "She never was much good at hearing news she didn't like."

"Mmm," I said, adjusting the angle of the laptop screen, ready to drop this conversation.

Still no movement outside.

Dad leant in closer, out of earshot of Soren. "What about you and Jordan?"

"That's not even—" I said, trying to ignore the conspiratorial grin on his face. "It's the end of the world, Dad. As if I have time for—"

I jumped up, sending the chair rolling away across the floor. Jordan had just walked on to the screen, glancing around at the bush, a rolled-up newspaper clutched in her right hand.

I leapt across to the panel on the wall and bashed the button to open the entrance.

"She's in," said Dad, a few seconds later, still watching the screen.

I hit the button again and raced up the hall to meet her. "Are you OK?" I asked, as soon as she came through the door. "What took so—?"

"I know why they're taking Mum and Georgia." She unrolled the newspaper, breathing hard, and turned to an article a few pages in.

The photos were the first clue that something was up. Two more stock portraits that had clearly been taken well before the article was written. They were of Mrs Lewis, the school librarian, and Amy, the insanely fast girl we'd last seen tearing into the darkness, away from Calvin and his men. The story underneath was just a couple of paragraphs reporting that Mrs Lewis and Amy were currently on their way to New Zealand for a literature summit.

I handed back the paper. "They got her."

"Yeah," said Jordan. "Her and Jeremy."

I nodded. No way was that a coincidence.

"Shackleton's weeding us out," said Jordan, lowering her voice so Kara and Soren wouldn't hear. "All of the – whatever we are. Everyone who's changing. They're getting rid of us. And Mum and Georgia are next."

Friday 3 July
41 days

"OK, here," said Jordan, flipping around the notepad she'd been scribbling on. "They were like this."

We were sitting on one of the couches in the living area, getting some space from Kara and Soren's bickering in the surveillance room. Dad had gone down to deliver Peter's dinner, along with a couple more old magazines we'd dug up.

I looked at the notepad. Jordan had drawn up a map of the town, with a bunch of red Xs marked out all across the north end. Cameras. Turned out *that* was what she'd been doing up there all that time yesterday: scouting around for a safe way into her house.

But, of course, there wasn't one.

"Doesn't look good," I said, pointing at the page. "Come in from this side and you get picked up by that one. Go in the front and you get caught here, and probably here too."

"What about the back fence?" said Jordan half-heartedly. "If we could get in from behind…"

"How? You'd have to get there first, and there'll be just as many cameras around the other side that we don't even know about yet."

Jordan sighed.

"Yeah," she said, closing up the notepad and dropping it on to the floor. "You're right. We'll just have to get in as quick as we can, and hope—"

I opened my mouth, but she held up a hand to stop me. "No, Luke – you don't want to come? Fine. But I'm not letting them take my family. I don't care if—"

"Jordan," I said, feeling that familiar anxiety, "I'll come. You know I will. If you decide to go up there, then we're going up together. But can we at least figure out if – I mean, do we actually have a *chance* here?"

Jordan stood up, staring at the ceiling.

"I don't know," she said. "That's not the point."

"Yes it is!" I said, getting up after her. "That's *exactly* the point, because if all we're going to do up there is die heroically, then—"

"Then at least we *tried!*" said Jordan, voice cracking. "At least we didn't just sit around and *wait* for it to happen! I have to. I have to do this. I can't just…"

She stepped forward and sort of crumpled into me, head on my shoulder, crying. I put my arms around her back and felt it jolt in time with her breathing. Jordan sniffed, tears soaking through my shirt.

She'd been threatening to melt down like this for days. I'd seen it coming. But that didn't make it any less miserable to watch. Any less terrifying. If Jordan lost her family, it would destroy her. And if that happened, it was all over. There was no way I could do this without her.

"We should head up while it's still dark," I said, caving in to the inevitable. "First thing in the morning, before…"

Jordan pulled away from me. She gazed at my face with an expression I couldn't read, and then—

She wrapped a hand around my head and pulled

me in and kissed me.

She was *right there* and I could see the wet streaks on her face and feel the pressure of her mouth and the brush of her tongue, and then she was breaking away again, pulling back, still face to face but not quite looking at me.

We stood there, neither of us speaking, and a few seconds later there was the sound of footsteps in the hallway.

We moved apart awkwardly just as Dad poked his head in through door, beaming. His smile faltered as he saw Jordan wiping her eyes. "Everything OK in here?"

"Yeah," she sniffed. "What's up?"

"The surveillance cameras," said Dad. "Soren's got them working again."

I glanced back at him, not really hearing, brain frozen at thirty seconds ago, replaying the moment on a loop. I wiped my mouth with the back of my hand.

"C'mon," said Jordan, jolting me back to reality, dragging me across to the surveillance room.

Most of the screens were still flashing error messages, but Kara and Soren were stooped over an image of the street outside Phoenix Mall.

"There are over three hundred angles on the

outside," Soren was telling her, "and probably as many more in the buildings." He punched the right arrow key as he spoke, and the screen jumped from camera to camera. "I will need to write something to categorise them all, and then—"

His finger froze, hovering above the key, and I looked down, forcing myself to focus.

We were looking out at the school. It was late afternoon, I realized, the sun drifting away behind the buildings. It was so hard to keep track of the time down here, without any natural light.

There were only a couple of lights on in the English block, and the playground was almost deserted. Almost. As we watched, two familiar figures skulked up to the building and tried the door.

Mike and Tank.

"They're checking the locker," said Jordan, closing in on Kara, voice still a bit choked. "Your locker. You're *still* communicating with them?"

"No," said Kara.

Soren went hastily back to tapping the keyboard, shifting our camera view away from the school. The screen flashed with images from the town centre.

Jordan looked like she was about to argue, but then her eyes flashed to the laptop and she shouted,

"Hey. Stop! Go back!"

Soren made a disgruntled noise, but started cycling back through the images we'd already seen.

"The one of the park," said Jordan. "With – *there*."

We were looking down on the playground. There was a woman sitting on a bench, right under the camera, a thick red pen in her hand and a stack of paper resting on her knee.

Peter's mum.

"What's she doing?" Jordan asked.

The top page on the stack was a giant clock face, with two wonky hands that looked like they'd been drawn on by a kid. Mrs Weir drew two new hands in over the top, scribbled *5 a.m.* in underneath, then initialled and dated the bottom of the page. She held the pile of papers up into the air, admiring it, then shuffled the top sheet to the back, revealing another identical clock on the next one.

"Marking homework or something," I said.

Jordan pushed Soren's chair away for a better look at the screen. Soren grunted again, but he didn't shove back.

We watched as Mrs Weir marked the next few pages. She went slowly, clearly in no hurry to finish.

Jordan squinted. "She keeps writing four-seven

underneath. That's not today's date. That's—"

"Tomorrow," I said.

Mrs Weir finished the next page and held it up into the air again. Five a.m. tomorrow.

"This is for us," I said. "I think – I think Peter's mum and dad are calling a meeting."

Chapter 22

**Saturday 4 July
40 days**

I pulled up the zip on my jumper, yawning, just awake enough to realize how bad it smelled. We'd definitely need to track down a laundry soon if we didn't all want to die of some gross skin disease.

It was just after 4.30 a.m. Dad's alarm had gone off a few minutes ago, and I'd rolled off the couch to find Jordan already up and dressed. She'd gone to check on Peter while the two of us got changed, just needing to give herself something to do, I think.

We were going to find her parents right after we met with Peter's.

Neither of us had talked about the *thing* that

had happened yesterday. But I'd been thinking. I'd definitely given it plenty of thought.

She was emotional. That's what I'd been telling myself. *It was just this impulsive, emotional thing that happened. Don't read too much into it.*

But it wasn't nothing. And even though I'd come up with a really good list of reasons why nothing was ever going to happen (like, for example, the end of the world and the fact that Peter would probably kill me), I was still thinking about it.

"Who are you?" asked Dad from across the room.

"Huh?" I said, snapping out of it.

Dad smiled. "*You.* How can you be so calm about this? What happened to my son, the panic merchant?"

"He's still here, trust me. But I've been almost dying since we arrived. You get – well, not *used* to it, but…" I shrugged. "And, hey, this time it might even be good news."

"Optimism!" said Dad as Jordan reappeared, carrying a couple of dirty plates. "From *my son!* Jordan, is this your influence?"

Jordan smiled feebly and went into the kitchen.

"How's Peter?" I called, trying to ignore the grin on Dad's face.

"Stuffing around on his computer." Jordan

dumped the plates into the sink and came back to join us. "You ready?"

"You always ask that like it's possible," I said.

We crossed to the surveillance room for one last look at the cameras. Since they hadn't told us anywhere else, we were guessing that the Weirs wanted to meet us at their house.

Our plan was to wait across the road in the bush and see if we could get their attention. They knew about the cameras, so surely they weren't expecting us to just stroll up to the front door. But if that didn't work... Well, rescuing Jordan's family was already a suicide mission, so why not cram two into one morning?

We found Kara waiting for us in the surveillance room. She stared straight at me, a weird, searching look on her face.

"Here to make sure we don't break anything?" said Jordan.

Kara didn't take her eyes off me. "I'm just very curious to see how this morning turns out."

"What's that meant to mean?"

"I don't suppose you'd believe me if I told you I was concerned for Luke's safety?" Kara asked.

"No," said Jordan, almost cracking a smile. "I

don't suppose I would."

All the laptops on the table were back in action now. Soren had set each one automatically cycling through the cameras in a different section of town.

I leant over an image of Peter's street. It was dark. No signs of life.

The camera angle shifted, closer to the Weirs" house. Nothing. Were they even—?

The surveillance picture flickered. Off, then on again. And then it was gone completely, replaced by a blur of static.

What?

I stood back. It was the same on every computer.

"What did you do?" Jordan snapped.

But Kara was looking just as confused as we were. She ran for the door. *"Soren!"*

"Have they found us?" I asked, checking the camera over the entrance. "If Calvin's figured out they've hijacked his security cameras…"

But there was no-one at the entrance.

Kara came tearing back into the room, dragging a barely-awake Soren behind her. He took one look at the computers and swore groggily.

"Why have we lost the signal?" Kara demanded, pushing him forward.

Soren stumbled over to the desk, brushing the sleep from his eyes. "We haven't…"

"Wake up!" barked Kara. "I don't have time for"

"I *am* awake!" said Soren. "Do you see an error message? We have not lost the signal. That static *is* the signal. We are seeing everything they're seeing. The whole network's gone offline."

A few minutes later, Jordan, Dad and I were jogging through the bush.

This couldn't be just a coincidence. The network hadn't just *happened* to go offline, fifteen minutes before we were meant to be meeting Peter's parents.

So how in the world had they done it?

As usual, Jordan was a couple of paces in front of us. She stopped walking and turned around. "I'm not coming," she whispered. "You two see what Peter's parents want. I have to go get my family."

She folded her arms, clearly expecting an argument. But I already knew there'd be no talking her out of this.

"Yeah," I said. "Go. We'll meet you back down there."

She moved to leave, hesitated, then turned back, pulling me in for a hug. I squeezed her back, and whatever Dad might say about me being *calm,* I wasn't. I was terrified.

Jordan loosened her grip, drawing back to look at me, and for a second, I thought maybe she was going to—

But no. Not this time. She released me and disappeared into the shadows.

I waited until she was out of sight. "Come on," I told Dad, "let's get this over with."

We walked the last few metres to the edge of the bush. The bits of splintered wood had been cleared away from Peter's front lawn by now, but there was still a gaping hole in the verandah. It wasn't like the Co-operative to leave something like that unrepaired. They usually jumped right on top of anything that poked a hole in their picture-perfect facade.

"All right," I said, checking the street one last time. "Ready?"

"OK," said Dad, giving me a nervous pat on the back. "Right behind you."

I sprinted out across the dirt and over the bike path, straight through the sights of at least one of the security cameras. Peter's front door was open before we were halfway up the lawn.

"Oh, thank goodness," said Mrs Weir, standing

aside as we bolted through. "We didn't know whether you even— Where's Peter?"

"He's safe," I said. "Don't worry."

Mrs Weir nodded, closing the door behind us. But she stayed at the window, eyes flashing across the yard like she was still waiting for someone.

"Who's this?" Peter's dad asked warily, coming in from the dining room.

"My dad," I said. "Jack. He's just arrived."

"Just arrived?" said Mrs Weir, and I cringed at the surge of hope in her voice.

"Yeah, but he isn't – it's not—"

Mr Weir rolled his wheelchair out past the window, into the faint glow of the streetlight, and I gasped. He was all red and purple, lips cracked, right eye swollen almost completely shut.

"Nice to meet you, Jack," he said, holding out a hand. Then, to me: "As you can see, Mr Shackleton is pretty keen to know where you guys are hiding out."

I shivered. "Mr Weir—"

"Looks worse than it is," he said dismissively, spinning his chair back toward the dining room. But he pulled up short as someone else stepped into the doorway.

At first, I didn't even believe it was her. My brain

chased itself around in a circle, trying to make sense of it.

"*Mum?*"

She pushed past Mr Weir, straight up to Dad.

"Emily…" Dad breathed.

"What are you doing here?" she demanded, like he'd come just to be difficult.

"What's *he* doing here?" I said, reeling. "What are *you*—?"

"He's coming!" said Mrs Weir, staring across the lawn. She moved back to the door, letting surprise guest number two into the house: Dr Montag.

He skidded to a stop, breathing like he'd run halfway across town to get here. He caught sight of Dad, and I saw the comprehension creep across his face. "You."

Montag spun around to Mum for an explanation, but she just threw up her hands. *What are you looking at me for?*

"Is this him?" Dad asked me. I could hear the cold anger waiting just beneath the surface.

My jaw clenched. "Yeah."

Mum was still fuming at Dad, like this whole morning was perfectly fine and normal except for him showing up.

"What is this?" I asked Mr Weir. "What are we doing here? Wait." I turned back to Montag, figuring it out. "*You* organized this?"

"Doctor Montag came to me at school," said Mrs Weir. "He told me your mother was in danger. He's trying to help her."

"We've only got about five minutes," said Montag. "I need you to listen to me."

"I'm not listening to *anything* you—"

"Shackleton has your blood samples," Montag pressed on, shutting me up instantly. "Within a couple of hours, he'll discover the truth about you and your mother."

"What truth?" asked Mum. Clearly, Montag hadn't bothered to fill her in on any of this ahead of time.

"That we're not supposed to be here," I said. "That he's free to kill us the next time he—"

"Luke can explain when you're safe," said Montag. His gaze flitted across the street, then back to me. "Take her to wherever you're staying. Keep her hidden."

"It's a trap," said Dad. He looked to me for confirmation. "Right? What's to keep him from following us back?"

"Luke, this is our only chance at keeping your mother alive," said Montag. "I've shut down the security cameras, but they'll be back online any time now. As soon as that happens—"

Montag broke off. His pocket was buzzing. He reached down and pulled out his mobile phone.

"Rob!" said Mum, and I realized it was the first time she'd seen a working phone in two months. "How—?"

"Not now," I hissed.

Montag looked down at the display, and his expression turned suddenly anxious. He motioned us all to keep quiet, then slid the phone open. "Yes?"

A pause. The doc's eyes widened. "*Now?* Don't be— We have a schedule. Her next appointment is—"

Another pause. The voice on the other end definitely wasn't happy.

"Yes, but that's still five days from now!" said Montag, eyes flashing to the window again.

The caller shot back even louder this time, and I realized who it was. Realized what they were talking about.

Montag mouthed an obscenity. "All right. Yes, fine, but I'm meeting you there. If anything happens to that child – no. No, I'm on my way."

I was tearing out the door before he'd even hung up the phone.

Calvin was coming for Jordan's family.

Chapter 23

I leapt down the front steps.

"Luke!" yelled Dad, racing out after me, Montag right behind him.

"Get them out of here!" I called back, wheeling around. "And don't let *him* see where."

He stopped running. "Where are you going?"

"Dad, *please!*"

A second of indecision. Then Dad turned back and threw a flying punch into Montag's face, sending him tripping back into the house.

"Jack!" yelled Mum, outraged.

I ran. Out on to the street, looking wildly around

for guards. No-one in sight. But that just meant they weren't standing under the streetlights.

Three blocks to Jordan's house.

I looked left, dashing across the first side-street, and for a few seconds, I could see straight down to the security centre at the end of the block. Nothing moving down there.

A voice behind me. I glanced back. Montag was tearing up the street, hand to his ear again. Back on the phone.

Two blocks to go.

I looked over my shoulder again. A dark shape darted across the road behind us, and then another, visible for just a second as they skirted the edge of a streetlight. Dad up front, lumbering along with Mr Weir across his back. Mrs Weir hurrying after him, and—

Clank, clank, clank, clank.

Noise up ahead. Running footsteps and jangling metal. Faint, but not for long. It was coming from around the next corner.

No.

Clank, clank, clank, clank.

A shout from the side-street.

Officer Calvin, a block away, flanked by four

security guards, all carrying the same semi-automatic weapons they'd been using when they went out into the bush, looking for Dad. Calvin was snarling into his phone.

I hit Jordan's block and, for a moment, the guards were out of sight. But I could still hear the clanking of their weapons, and the pounding of their feet, and the fierce back-and-forth of Calvin and Montag's phone conversation as they closed in on each other.

I swerved sideways as a gleaming black pole sprang up out of nowhere. One of the new cameras. A little green light blinked out from the dome at the top. The security network was back online.

Not that I had panic to spare for that right now.

I jumped the fence, into Jordan's yard. Up the steps and through the open front door. "JORDAN!"

Jordan's mum was standing at the foot of the stairs, still in her pyjamas, arm wrapped tightly around a panicked-looking Georgia. I swear, Mrs Burke's stomach had doubled in size since the last time I'd seen her. She opened her mouth, almost screaming as I came into the room, but then saw who I was.

Jordan came thundering down the stairs. "What? Are they—?"

"They're coming!" I said. "Where's your dad?"

"Upstairs! He's just—"

"No, Jordan – they're coming *now!*"

Jordan swayed, grabbing the banister, and for a horrible second I thought she was slipping into another vision. But she steadied herself, taking the rest of the stairs in three strides. "Out the back!" she panted, holding her mum's arms. "Get over the fence and *run*. Into the bush, deep as you can—"

"Over the fence?" said Mrs Burke weakly, free hand drifting to her belly. "Jordan, I don't think I can—"

"Just *do it!*" Jordan shouted. She started dragging them toward the hall, shooting a desperate glance up at the second-floor landing. "DAD! GET DOWN HERE!"

There was a bang as someone kicked the gate open outside.

Georgia started to cry. She buried her face in her mum's side and her soccer cap fell to the carpet.

"Don't worry, sweetheart," whispered Mrs Burke, starting up the hall. "Jordan's going to take us—"

Georgia screamed.

Mrs Burke opened her mouth to calm her down, but whatever she was going to say got swallowed up in a rush of feet pounding on to the verandah.

They were here.

Chapter 24

Calvin swept into the room and stabbed a red-gloved hand at Georgia and her mum. Two of his men raced forward – Coffee Cart Guard, bandaged and bruised, and a curly-haired officer I thought I'd seen stacking shelves at the supermarket once.

"RUN!" Jordan shouted, pushing her mum toward the back door and moving to head off the guards.

Calvin pointed his last remaining officer up the stairs.

Wait a sec...

Weren't there four guards before?

The curly-haired officer clamped down on Jordan's

shoulders and tried to shove her aside. Jordan grabbed him back, her heels digging into the carpet.

"Stop!" screamed Mrs Burke. "Let her go!"

"Mum, please!" Jordan begged. "Go! Before—"

BANG.

The back door smashed open and Officer Barnett came bounding in from the other end of the hall, blocking the only escape we had left.

"All clear, Chief," he reported, clutching his rifle in both hands, looking like he was having the time of his life.

Calvin nodded in Jordan's direction. "Deal with her, will you?"

Jordan was still locked in her wrestling match with the other guard. Barnett got around the back of her and smashed the butt of his weapon down behind her knees. She cried out, releasing the guard and dropping halfway to the ground. Barnett kicked her the rest of the way over and planted his boot down between her shoulder blades.

I took a step toward them, but then Calvin hoisted up his weapon, aiming it at my chest, disintegrating whatever shred of hope I had left. "A bit late for heroics, Mr Hunter."

Montag stood in the doorway, eyeing Calvin's

gun. "Are those really necessary?"

Calvin didn't even look at him.

Coffee Cart Guard had both hands on Jordan's mum now, but he was still struggling to get her under control. The curly-haired officer was clutching Georgia around the middle, trying to pull her away. Georgia shrieked at him to leave her alone. Mrs Burke aimed a knee up between the curly-haired guard's legs and he crumpled, grabbing himself.

"Oi!" Barnett shouted, swinging his weapon around and pointing it at Jordan's mum. "That'll do."

Mrs Burke stopped struggling. The two recruits stepped back, raising their rifles, like they'd only just remembered they had them. Georgia cowered behind her mum.

"Get them out," Calvin ordered, rolling his eyes. "And *don't*—"

A spray of weapons fire exploded above our heads, impossibly loud, like the whole house was coming down on top of us.

Georgia screamed again.

"DAD!" Jordan strained under Barnett's boot, her face contorted with terror like I'd never seen before.

Calvin looked back to Coffee Cart Guard and the other guy. "Out!"

They started dragging Jordan's mum towards the door.

"NO!" Jordan shouted, tears pouring down now. "YOU'RE *NOT*—!"

Barnett jabbed his rifle down into the back of her head. "*Shut up.*"

I ran at him, no idea what I was doing. Almost instantly, a solid mass slammed into my back, throwing me to the ground. I hit the carpet and someone grabbed me by the hair.

"I'll get to you in a minute," Calvin growled behind my ear. He dropped my head roughly, still pinning me down with one knee.

The two young guards hauled Mrs Burke and Georgia to the door, and Montag stepped aside to let them out.

Georgia was howling so much she could barely breathe. "Leave me alone!" she gasped. "No! I don't want to go down there!"

Down there? I thought dimly. It wasn't the first time Georgia seemed to know more than she should have.

She took a choking breath as they reached the verandah, and let out another ear-destroying scream.

Surely the whole street had to be up by now.

Calvin's knee dug into my spine. I was shaking, fear like a freight train, waiting for him to hurry up and—

SMASH!

Something shattered upstairs. There was a strangled shout, and a thump, and then Jordan's dad came sprinting into view, clutching the other guard's rifle in one hand.

Calvin twisted around, taking aim at him. "Drop it."

Mr Burke froze halfway down the stairs, but held on to the rifle, hands trembling as Georgia's wails faded away down the street.

"*Chief,*" said Montag, eyes flashing. "We've got what we came for."

"Yes," said Calvin. "You can go now, Rob."

"Do you think we can just walk away from this? You've already woken up half the town, Bruce. Noah's orders—"

Calvin's left hand blurred above my head, leaving his rifle and drawing the pistol from his holster. He pointed it at Montag. "You can *go* now, Rob."

Everyone stopped. Barnett raised his weapon slightly, but didn't seem to know where to point it.

Jordan caught my eye.

"Bruce," Montag shook his head. "You're not going to— How do you think Noah's going to react when he finds out—?"

Jordan stretched out the fingers on her left hand. *Five seconds.* I cringed, but started counting down.

"When he finds out you were tragically caught in the crossfire as we took down Hunter and Burke?" said Calvin, grinning horribly. "Yes, I imagine he'll be quite upset. But I'm sure Dr Galton will be able to pick up—"

Barnett shouted in surprise as Jordan jerked sideways, rolling out from under him. He pointed his rifle down again, but she was already throwing herself into the back of his legs, dropping him to the ground.

Jordan's dad flew down the stairs.

"Hey—!"

I twisted around, punching Calvin right in the groin. He grunted violently, and the air above my head blasted apart as he fired his rifle. There was a strangled shout from the stairs.

"Dad!" gasped Jordan, twisting under Barnett, who was sprawled on top of her now.

But it wasn't Mr Burke. The other guard – the one who'd disappeared upstairs – was up on the landing, gazing down at himself, like he still wasn't sure what had happened. Then his legs gave out and he went crashing down the stairs.

Jordan's dad leapt over him, horrified, and pounded down the rest of the stairs.

Calvin was doubled over, more worried about his own pain than the officer he'd just shot. I scrambled away from him. Too late. Calvin let the rifle fall to his waist and raised his pistol again. I shrank back, shielding myself with my hands. Something blurred over my head.

Calvin cried out and sprawled sideways as Jordan's dad screamed past, swinging the fallen guard's rifle like a baseball bat.

SMACK!

The pistol slipped out of Calvin's hand.

I steeled myself and charged at him, before I had the chance to talk myself out of it. We crashed back into the wall. Somewhere across the room, I heard Barnett cry out in pain as Mr Burke moved in to help Jordan.

My right hand slipped up to Calvin's head and came away sticky with blood.

"*Luke!*" Jordan yelled. "Put your hand in his mouth!"

Wha—?

But then my mind flashed back to Calvin's bizarre freak-out at the airport. *Oh.*

I put my bloodied hand to Calvin's face, clawing at his mouth, trying to force open his clenched jaw.

He grabbed at his rifle, feet flailing as he pushed back up into a standing position. I threw down my other hand, trying to keep the weapon pinned to his stomach, but he was too strong.

My fingers slid over Calvin's face, drawing bloody trails down his cheeks. He gave up on the rifle, shoving me with both hands, knocking me back to the carpet.

Jordan's hands grabbed me from behind. "Luke – *come on!*"

I looked up at Calvin. He was staring back, shivering with—

With what?

Fear?

"Barnett!" he called shakily.

Across the room, Barnett was struggling to his feet. "Sir?"

"Stand down," Calvin ordered, pressing closer to the wall. "We're not—" He took a shuddering breath. "Stand down."

Jordan gave my jumper another tug and I got up.

She was sobbing.

"Chief—" Barnett's rifle was gone, but he reached for his pistol.

"No!" said Calvin. "Please. Drop your weapon."

Please? I thought dizzily, edging toward the door.

"Do it," said Mr Burke, still brandishing his rifle at Barnett like a club, completely confused at Calvin's sudden change of heart.

Barnett threw up his hands. The pistol thudded to the carpet. Mr Burke backed away from him, joining Jordan and me at the door.

Montag was on the stairs, tending to the injured guard. He peered at Calvin like he was seeing something we weren't. Then his gaze fell on the three of us. "What are you waiting for? *Go!*"

I backed through the door. As soon as we were out-side, Mr Burke turned and ran.

"Wait!" I called. "We need to—"

But he was already sailing over the fence.

The next-door neighbours stared, open-mouthed, from their front porch. There were others too, crouching behind fences or leaning out their upstairs windows.

"Where did they go?" Mr Burke called. "Which way?"

The neighbours shrank back, no idea whose side they were supposed to be on.

"Mr Burke!" I said, running out after him. "We can't!"

He walked into the middle of the street, dark eyes shifting from neighbour to neighbour. *"WHICH WAY?"*

Jordan overtook me, shuddering with tears. "Dad!"

Mr Burke darted around the corner to meet her. The two of them took off, back towards Peter's place, and I realized Jordan wasn't heading for safety. She was running in the direction that the guards had been going in her vision. I took off after them.

On a good day, Jordan is easily faster than me. But this was not a good day. She was borderline hysterical now, and it was slowing her down.

I heard shouts from the other end of the street. A whole new batch of guards. I threw out a hand, catching the edge of Jordan's jumper. Mr Burke kept running, oblivious.

"Let *go!*" Jordan stumbled forward, like she'd just drag me along behind her if she had to.

"No," I said, holding tight. "Call your dad back!"

She jerked sideways, trying to shake me. "Go, then! Go! Just get out of—"

"You're coming with me," I said, grabbing her arm with my other hand.

"Let go!"

"The cameras are back on! And those guards are going to be here in—"

"I don't care!"

"Jordan—"

"Stop! I'm not—"

"YOU CAN'T SAVE THEM!"

And for a second, she stopped fighting.

Behind her, I saw Mr Burke wheel around and start coming back.

"I – *have* – to!" Jordan choked.

"You can't," I said. "Not like this. Not if it means—"

Mr Burke thundered up to us. He reached out to tear me away from Jordan.

"WHAT ARE YOU DOING?" he shouted, almost as distraught as she was. "LEAVE HER!"

"No – Dad—" Jordan el bowed him away.

I let her go. She stayed put, breathing hard, throwing another glance at the approaching guards with a look on her face that made me feel like my chest was caving in.

Jordan grabbed her dad around the wrist. She gave a spluttering cough and dragged him away into the bush.

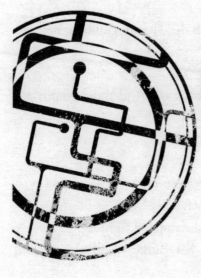

Chapter 25

Back underground. Back down the dark, spongy stairs, Jordan's shaky breath rasping in my ears the whole way.

Security had been only metres away when the entrance sealed shut above our heads. I just hoped it had still been dark enough to keep them from seeing where we'd disappeared to.

I heard confused voices downstairs. So Dad and the others were safe, at least.

I raced through to the surveillance room and found Dad huddled over the computer image of the entrance. Kara was leaning down behind him, holding a bloodied scalpel. I panicked for half a second, then realized what was going on. She was dealing with Mr Weir's suppressor.

"We OK?" I asked, pushing past Soren. Something was nagging at me, fighting for my attention, but I couldn't work out what it was.

"Yes," said Dad in a weirdly hollow voice. "I think so."

I looked down and saw a couple of guards racing under the camera, into the bush.

Kara turned as Jordan and her dad came in. For a second, I thought I saw a flicker of sympathy, but then she pursed her lips and said, "Oh, good. Another visitor." She held up her scalpel. "Does he have one too?"

"No," I said hurriedly. "Just Mr Weir."

Kara ducked back into the lab.

Jordan ignored her, running a ring around the table, trying to take in every screen at once. *"Where are they?"*

"Here!" I said, spotting them. Jordan and Mr Burke loomed up behind me.

An unmarked door, out the back of the medical centre. Coffee Cart Guard was pushing Mrs Burke and Georgia inside. The curly-haired guard stood behind, rifle raised at their backs.

Ten seconds later, they were gone. Jordan collapsed on the desk. Mr Burke backed silently away from the screen, clutching the rifle in his hand even tighter.

I moved closer to Jordan, head spinning, still dizzy with adrenalin, no clue what to do for her. I put my hand on her back and she slumped down across my lap.

"I'm going to go and get dressed," Soren announced, oblivious as ever. He left the room.

I glanced over at Dad, and I realized what had been nagging at me. It was like someone had just plunged a knife into my gut.

"Where's Mum?" I asked.

Jordan looked up.

Dad opened his mouth to answer and I realized that he didn't need to, that the hollowness in his voice before was answer enough. "She's not here," he said. "I tried, but she wouldn't— She wouldn't come with me. She's still back at the house."

"She'll be OK," said Jordan. "Montag'll look after her."

"Jordan, we've already—" I almost tripped as she shifted her grip on the bed frame we were carrying. "The whole reason Montag called us up there was because he *couldn't* look after her anymore."

I lifted up my end of the bed, angling it around, and we finally got it in through the doorway. We lugged the rusty frame across Kara and Soren's living room and set it down against the wall.

We'd spent the last half-hour or so converting this place into another bedroom. Dad, Jordan and I had still been crashing on the couches every night, but now that there were nine of us down here, we'd decided it was time to work out some more permanent sleeping arrangements. As much as anything, I think we just needed something mindless to do.

The eight hours since we'd come back underground had felt like a movie I'd watched while I was half asleep. Like my brain had called a time-out and refused to take anything more in.

Jordan wiped the grime off her hands and sat down on the edge of the bed. "At least your mum's got *someone* looking out for her."

"So does yours," I said, coming around to join her. "As soon as we find a way into the medical centre—"

"Yeah," said Jordan, and it was enough to tell me she didn't want to go over it all again.

Once the initial panic of the morning had settled down a bit, Dad had dragged Jordan and me into the kitchen and forced us to eat something. By the time we'd finished, we'd both pulled ourselves together a bit.

Still, it didn't take Jordan long to get into another shouting match with Kara. This time, it was the suppressors. When we'd first got back this morning, Kara had shut Mr Weir's suppressor down without actually removing it, just like she'd done with ours. But then, somehow, Jordan convinced her it was about time she got us all back on the operating table and got rid of them completely.

It was possible that "somehow" was Jordan's dad looming over Kara through the whole conversation. Mr Burke was in there now, keeping an eye on Mr Weir while she did the surgery.

I watched Jordan out of the corner of my eye. She was wearing the shirt I'd had on the day Mum and I arrived in Phoenix. One of the few things I still owned from the outside world. Clothing options were pretty limited down here, so I'd given her some stuff from the bag Montag had packed me. It was totally a practical decision, but it changed the way I looked at her. Or maybe that wasn't the clothes.

Jordan turned to face me. She didn't say anything. She just fixed me with that same barely-holding-it-together expression she'd been wearing all day.

I wanted to do something. Hold her hand. Put my arm around her. *Something.* I wanted it to be simple. But there was nothing simple about any of this.

I leant forward. The springs from the mattress were starting to dig into my legs. "I hate this," I sighed.

Jordan bit her lip, like I'd said something wrong. "What?"

"All this," I said, waving a hand at the makeshift bedroom. "Moving beds out of storage. It feels too much like – I don't know. Like we're settling in."

"Yeah," said Jordan, shoulders relaxing slightly. "Well, better down here than up there." She stood up. "Come on. One more bed."

We headed back into Kara's room. What used to be Kara's room, anyway. She'd reluctantly agreed to move her stuff in with Soren so that Peter's parents could have some space to themselves.

More beds were piled up against the back wall, unused for years since the original team had abandoned the place.

"We should go see Peter later," said Jordan, hauling one of them down. "Fill him in on everything."

I nodded, taking the other end.

"We could even—" Jordan hesitated. "*Couldn't*

223

we let him out for a while? He should be in an OK mood, right? Now that he knows his parents are safe."

"Yeah. Maybe."

The Weirs had spent most of the morning in Peter's room. Mrs Weir was still down there with Dad. We'd explained the situation to them – as much as we *could* explain, anyway – and they'd both seen what he'd done to those guards back at their house, so they'd agreed to let us keep holding him there for now. But I could tell that was a conversation we'd have more than once. Especially after Peter told them it was Kara and Soren who'd abducted him in the first place.

We pulled the bed away from the wall. "Hey…" I murmured. "What's that?"

There was something poking out from behind the stack of beds. An architectural drawing in a black frame. I dropped the bed and dragged out the frame, setting it down on the mattress.

Jordan picked up a crusty rag off the floor and wiped away some of the dust.

It was a floor plan of the whole Vattel Complex, from back when it was all still intact. Four buildings, spaced apart in a diagonal line, connected by long passageways. "This is where we are," said Jordan, pointing to a room in the second building, labelled

FEMALE SLEEPING QUARTERS. "Module B."

"So Peter is somewhere in here, right?" I said, sliding my finger across to Module C, the biggest of the four buildings. Definitely a research facility, but there was nothing to indicate what the research actually *was*. "And then there's this whole other building we haven't even been to yet."

"And another one back … Hang on," said Jordan, finger hovering over the words MODULE A— PRIMARY POWER GENERATOR. "If this is…"

She stared up at the ceiling, visualising something. "The crater," she whispered. "I knew *something* must have happened down here to create that thing—"

"Taking an inventory of my things now, are we?" said Kara, walking in behind us.

"Yep." Jordan turned around, not missing a beat. "That's not a problem, is it?"

Kara looked over her glasses at her. "Jordan, you are about to be facedown on my operating table. This is not the moment to test my patience."

Jordan looked like she had another comeback ready to fire, but a burst of laughter from the hallway shut the conversation down.

Peter's dad came leaping in to join us, almost crashing into the doorway on his way through. I almost didn't recognise him without the wheelchair. He did a wild, stumbling lap of the room, bracing against the walls a couple of times to keep from falling over, shouting and punching the air like tearing around the room was the most awesome thing in the whole world.

"Where's Jess?" he asked, grinning like a crazy person despite the pain it must have caused to his battered face. "Where is my beautiful wife?"

Kara sighed, almost smiling, like she couldn't believe she'd let this riff-raff into her home. She waved a hand in the direction of Peter's room, and Mr Weir headed for the door again, practically skipping.

"Jess!" he bellowed, flying away down the hall. "Pete! Come on! Look at this!"

And despite all the other crap that should have been weighing on me, I couldn't help laughing at the sound of him rampaging away down the corridor. Even Jordan managed a smile.

Kara flicked something off the front of her coat. "Well then," she said. "Who's next?"

Finally, the day was over. I lay on my side with my eyes shut, painfully exhausted but nowhere near sleep. Thinking about everything without actually thinking about anything.

I traced a finger over the fresh row of stitches at the base of my spine. I'd expected to feel some kind of relief at finally being rid of Shackleton's tracking device, but mostly I just felt numb.

I guess I had bigger things to worry about.

Across the room, Jordan's dad was snoring. I had no idea what time it was, but I'd been lying here for what felt like forever.

Kara and Soren were the only ones still up; I'd heard them whispering to each other in the hall a few minutes ago. But then, they were also the only ones who hadn't almost died today.

I opened my eyes again. I could just make out Jordan's face resting on her pillow, a metre away. Impossibly peaceful. I watched her body rise and fall with her breathing, and found myself thinking again about what had happened between us yesterday.

Trying to figure out *what* I thought about it. Trying not to think about how Peter would react if he knew.

In the end, we hadn't made it in to see him today. By the time Kara had got our suppressors out, it was late afternoon, which had given us just enough time for a pre-dinner screening of the Tabitha DVD for Mr Burke and the Weirs. Neither of us had felt like we had the energy for another argument with Peter after that.

Tomorrow, I told myself. Put it on the to-do list. Somewhere between "wash underpants" and "save humanity".

Jordan rolled over in her sleep, and I closed my eyes.

Before we did anything else tomorrow, we should sit everyone down and compare notes. See if Peter's parents or Jordan's dad knew anything that might—

A distant, echoing crash rang out from somewhere way off across the complex, shattering my last hope of falling asleep.

I was already halfway out of bed when I heard Soren's petrified scream.

Chapter 26

"Jordan!" I hissed, jolting her shoulder. "Jordan, get up!"

Her eyes snapped open. "What's happening?"

"I don't know," I said, turning to shake Dad awake. "Something down the hall. I heard—"

Another heavy smash echoed up the corridor.

"That," I finished.

I ran to the door. The lights were still on at the end of the hall, but whatever was happening, it was coming from deeper inside the complex.

Soren screamed again, and there was a sound like breaking concrete.

The Co-operative? Had Shackleton finally figured out where we were?

"Come on!" I said, heart thudding, as the others dragged themselves out of bed. I raced out the door, just as a new sound cut through all the smashing.

Peter, bellowing like he was being tortured.

I sprinted down the hallway, still no idea whether he was the cause or the victim of whatever was going on down there – or which would be worse.

The light at the end of the corridor cast a jumble of shadows over the shrapnel jutting out from the walls. If I wasn't careful, I was going to slice myself open before we even got there.

I could hear Dad behind me, barrelling to catch up. "What's going on?" he asked.

"I— *Whoa!*" I grunted, dodging just in time to avoid impaling myself on a spike of wood. "I dunno."

A dark shape appeared up ahead, silhouetted in the light at the end of the hallway. I pulled up, half-expecting to be torn apart by gunfire. But it wasn't security.

Soren came flying up the corridor toward us, a murderous look on his face. He was carrying one of the steel bars from across Peter's door.

"Hey!" I shouted.

But he just shoved past and kept running.

Soren glanced back over his shoulder, face catching the light for a second, and I gasped. He had red gashes across both cheeks, like he'd been clawed by an animal.

Kara backed into view further down the hallway, at the place where it widened out in front of Peter's room. She was clutching another one of the steel bars, swinging it up over her shoulder.

"Tell me where she is!" yelled Peter, just out of sight.

OK, I thought, closing in on them, *not a Cooperative problem.*

Kara ducked to the ground as a steel chair – *my* steel chair – came flying at her head. The chair smashed against the wall behind her and rebounded, skittering up the corridor toward me. I jumped it, almost tripping, and stumbled out into a warzone.

The floor was covered in battered books and little foam beanbag balls and whatever else Peter had been able to lay his hands on. His desk was on its side in the middle of the floor, its legs bent out of shape. And, somehow, the old leather couch was lying upside-down across the room, blocking the hallway at the other end.

Kara was back at Peter's doorway. She took a

couple of heavy breaths, trying to get back some shred of her usual composure. "If you think this kind of behaviour is going to – *Peter!* No, do not—"

Peter let out a furious roar, and suddenly he was bursting through the doorway, driving his bookcase out in front of him like a battering ram. He smashed into Kara, knocking her to the concrete, and then hurled what was left of the bookcase across the floor.

Dad came up from behind me, moving to grab Peter, but I held out a hand to stop him.

"No," I murmured, "let me." I edged into the middle of the room, arms outstretched. "Hey … Peter…"

"Where is she?" he shouted, clawing the hair back out of his eyes, fingernails dark with blood. *"Where's Jordan?"*

"She's—" I broke off, glancing back up the corridor. Where *was* Jordan?

"I do not respond well to tantrums, Peter," said Kara, pushing unsteadily to her feet. "If you wish to see Jordan again, go back into your room and we'll discuss the situation."

"WE'RE ALREADY BLOODY DISCUSSING IT!"

Peter grabbed the upturned desk by one leg and

heaved it up at Kara. She yelped as the desk slammed into her, staggered over the smashed bookcase and crumpled to the ground again.

"Peter, c'mon," I said, keeping what I hoped was a safe distance. "You don't need to—"

But Peter was already standing over Kara, holding the metal bar she'd dropped when the bookcase hit her. He raised it into the air above his head.

Kara twisted away from him. "Listen to me," she pleaded. "Peter, if you do this—"

"Stop!" called a voice from way back up the corridor. "Put it down!"

It was Jordan. Peter's head snapped up. He abandoned Kara instantly, turning toward the voice. The rod slipped out of his hand, thunking down an inch from Kara's face.

A figure blurred past me, out of the hallway. Now I realized who Jordan had *really* been yelling at.

Soren charged past, straight up to Peter, chest heaving, blood still trickling down his cheeks. He had a gun. The automatic rifle Jordan's dad had brought down from the surface.

Peter leapt back. "Hey – hey, no. Mate, that's not—"

"Get down!" Soren ordered, voice cracking,

twitching his weapon at the floor.

Peter dropped, facedown.

Soren's eyes flickered. "No, I meant – I meant kneel. Get on your knees!"

"*Stop!*" cried Jordan, running in. "Soren! Put it *down!*"

"I'll shoot him!" Soren shrieked, as Peter pushed himself shakily to his knees. "Any of you – any of you try anything, and I'll—"

"I thought you weren't a murderer!" I said desperately, jumping back up again. "Isn't that what you told me, back when—?"

Soren burst out laughing, sounding as unhinged as Peter. "Hunter, if you – you should be begging me to do this! If you knew what this – what this *friend* of yours was really capable of…"

"Put the gun down, Soren," croaked a voice from the floor. "This is not a solution."

Soren glanced down at Kara, who was slowly sitting up. "Mum! We can end this right now!"

"End *what?*" said Jordan. "How is this going to help anything?"

"Yeah," said Peter, nodding frantically. "Exactly."

"Quiet!" snapped Soren, shaking the rifle some more.

"Do you think killing him has never occurred to me?" said Kara, like this was just any normal mother-and-son argument. "If it were truly that simple, don't you think I would have done it already? We both know it doesn't work like that."

"No we *don't*." Soren stomped his foot. "You *think* you know how it works, but you're just—"

"You cannot undo what's already been done," said Kara, freeing herself from the splintered bookcase and clambering back to her feet. "And if we're to have even a *hope* of figuring all of this out—"

She stopped short at the sound of heavy feet pounding up the hallway. Mr Burke pulled up behind my dad, a silver auto-injector pen glinting in his hand.

Soren turned to look for a fraction of a second—

Which was all the time Peter needed to throw out his hands and grab the barrel of the rifle.

"HEY!" yelled Soren, fumbling with his end.

Peter jabbed the rifle like a spear, driving the butt of it back into Soren's chest. Soren grunted, fingers slipping, and Peter wrenched the weapon away from him. He flipped it around, wrapping his hands around the grips.

I took a panicked step back as Soren dropped to the floor. Peter raised the rifle.

"No!" shouted Jordan, running forward.

SMASH!

Peter smacked the gun down hard across his face. Soren collapsed, groaning.

Peter straightened up for another swing, but Jordan dived in and grabbed his arm. "That's enough!"

Peter wheeled around, red-faced. And suddenly, Jordan was rocketing across the ground, tumbling over herself, slamming into the overturned desk and bringing it sliding along the floor with her, crashing to a stop against the uneven wall.

Peter dropped the gun and ran over. "No! No, I didn't mean—!"

I grabbed him and shoved him backwards, a sudden violent strength surging through my body. He wrenched his shoulders, fighting to get free, but for a moment I was stronger.

"It was an accident," said Peter, horrified. "I thought she was – I thought it was *her*." He pointed back at Kara, who had picked up the rifle and was busy unloading it.

I didn't want to hear it. I shoved him back toward his room, not even worrying what he might do to me, just needing him out of the way.

"No, I need to talk to her!" He flailed desperately,

choking on his words. "I need to tell her it was—"

And then he was shouting and grabbing his leg. Dad had just swooped in out of nowhere, sticking Peter with Mr Burke's auto-injector.

Jordan grunted as her dad picked her up.

"Wait!" Peter lurched forward again, leg already starting to drag, and I almost let go of him. "Please – Mr Burke, you have to let me—"

"Come on, Luke." Dad grabbed Peter's arm and we pushed him back into what was left of his room.

"Please!" Peter cried again, as Mr Burke carried Jordan out into the hallway. "No – Jordan! JORDAN!"

He dissolved into tears, melting down completely. Dad threw the door shut. I held it just long enough for him to get the first barricade back into place, then ran after Jordan and her dad.

Chapter 27

"I'm so sorry," said Peter's mum, taking Jordan's hand in both of hers. "I don't know *where* this is coming from. Peter's not like this. He's a good boy. I know that's what every parent thinks about their own child, but—"

"Mrs Weir, please," said Jordan, "stop. I'm *fine*. Believe me, I've had worse."

That was true. But it shouldn't have been.

She should have been dead. That was Kara's assessment. The only reason Jordan was still here was that Peter's desk had hit the wall ahead of her, shielding her from the junk sticking out of the wall.

Kara had checked her out last night and found only a mild concussion and a few little scrapes and bruises. And given Jordan's freakish healing abilities, even those would probably be gone by tomorrow. Still, I couldn't even look at her without picturing all the ways last night *could* have ended.

Soren, meanwhile, had spent the whole morning skulking around the place, wincing at his scratched cheeks and bruised head, looking for someone to feel sorry for him.

The story he and Kara had given us was that they'd seen Peter trashing his room and gone in to "settle him down". I had a feeling they'd just leave him to it next time.

It was the afternoon now, and the eight of us – everyone except Peter – were in the surveillance room, around the table with all the laptops. Jordan wasn't about to let a little thing like almost getting skewered slow her down. She'd called us all together to start figuring out a way to get her mum back. To get *our* mums back, if mine was even still out there.

But so far, all we'd done was talk around in circles about last night.

Mr Weir had been pacing the room since he walked in. After finally getting his legs back, it was like he never wanted to sit down again.

"Can't blame yourself, Jess," he said, pausing behind Mrs Weir. "Pete's sick. Whatever this is, it's not – he's not just another one of your behaviour kids. You're not going to fix this one up with a sticker chart."

Mrs Weir nodded, close to tears. "I just wish someone could tell me *why* this is happening to him."

"Kara can," said Jordan abruptly.

"Sorry?" said Mr Weir.

Kara shot Jordan a look that would've made Mr Hanger jealous.

"She knows something," said Jordan, unfazed. "Don't you?"

The room fell silent, all eyes on Kara. I could see the gears turning in her head. Peter's parents knew all about last night, and Mr Weir was already calling for Kara and Soren to be locked up. This was not a good time to be difficult.

"Any answer I gave you would be almost entirely speculative," said Kara.

"Great," said Jordan. "Start speculating."

"No," Soren sneered. "We don't have to tell you any—"

Mr Burke laid a hand on his shoulder. "Let her talk."

Soren sank back down in his chair.

"All right," said Kara, folding her arms on the desk, determinedly calm. "The bushland above our heads. How old do you think it is?"

No-one answered. Mr Weir looked at her like he was sure she was wasting his time.

"A hundred years?" Kara prompted. "Two hundred?" She paused again, waiting for a response.

"Yes," said Mrs Weir, exasperated. "Yes, probably something like that."

"That would be a reasonable estimate," said Kara. "To all outward appearances, that forest *should* be centuries old. But that is not the case. Twenty years ago, this whole area was a barren wasteland."

"You're saying somebody planted it," said Dad. "The Shackleton Co-operative."

"No," said Kara. "Nobody planted it. It grew here naturally. Or, at least, it grew here without human effort. Somehow, this entire forest sprang up from nothing in a mere two decades."

Mr Weir began circling around the table toward Kara, clearly losing patience. "You're full of it."

"No," said Jordan slowly, like she was piecing something together. "I don't think she is."

I thought back to our trip out to the wall. "Barren

wasteland" pretty much summed up the land on the other side.

"What does any of that have to do with Peter?" asked Mrs Weir.

"It might have nothing to do with him," said Kara. "But it's possible that whatever is accelerating the growth of the bushland is having some kind of equivalent effect on Peter."

Fallout, I thought.

It took me a second to figure out why the word had suddenly popped into my head. A hazy memory from what felt like a million years ago. Hiding in Ketterley's office, hearing him worrying about "fallout" giving them a whole town full of Crazy Bills to deal with.

It was starting to look like maybe he was right.

Mr Weir stood over Kara. "What's that supposed to mean?"

"Your guess is as good as mine," said Kara, holding up her hands. "As I said, most of this is speculation."

I had a feeling our guess was nowhere near as good as hers, but it only took one look at Kara to tell me that was all she was planning on telling us – and one look at Mr Weir to tell me how quickly the meeting would implode if we kept pushing it.

And to be honest, right now I was more interested

in rescuing our families than I was in helping the guy who'd almost got Jordan killed.

"All right, look," I said, "even if that's all true, it doesn't really change much, does it?" I turned to Kara. "Not unless you actually have some way to help Peter."

Kara shook her head.

Mr Weir said something obscene under his breath. "Then why are we even *having* this conversation?"

"You didn't *ask* me for a solution," said Kara irritably, rolling her chair away from him. "You asked me to guess at the *cause* of Peter's condition, which I have done. Now, are we going to discuss the matter we came here to talk about, or are we going to degenerate into a brawl over a problem I have no power to solve?"

Mr Weir didn't answer right away. He seemed to be seriously weighing up the brawling option.

"Please, Mr Weir," said Jordan, indicating the empty chair next to Peter's mum.

Mr Weir rubbed his eyes. He circled back around the table, finally taking a seat. "OK," he said heavily, "let's get started. Like I said, Shackleton hasn't had much to say to me since he put me in that wheelchair, so all I really know is what they give me to write up for the paper. But it doesn't take insider information to see how much strain the security guys are under right now."

"Not for long, though," said Jordan.

"Right," said Mr Weir. "Calvin's recruiting. But, for the moment, that's also giving him a whole pack of new hassles to deal with, like how does he train them all? And how does he make sure they stay loyal when he starts asking them to do things they don't want to do?"

I nodded. In hindsight, probably the only reason we'd gotten out of Jordan's house alive was that half of Calvin's team had been new guys.

"Anyway, the upshot of all that is that Shackleton hasn't had a whole lot of manpower to spare, scouring the bush for you guys," Mr Weir said. "But that's not going to—"

"But how is it that the Shackleton Co-operative doesn't already know about this place?" Jordan's dad cut in. "It must stretch halfway under the town."

"Of *course* they know about it," grumbled Soren. "Who do you think Shackleton got this land from in the first place?"

"Then why haven't they—?"

"Because," said Kara, "as far as Noah Shackleton knows, this whole complex was completely filled in with concrete when my mother and her people left."

"Huh," said Mr Weir. "I guess that'd be why Ketterley was always complaining about *obstructions* when the town was being built."

"What about the giant *crater* in the middle of the bush?" asked Jordan. "That didn't raise a few eyebrows?"

"Yes, well, that tunnel's been sealed off now," said Kara. She glanced disapprovingly at Soren, who glowered back at her.

I stared down at the surveillance image in front of me. Kids from school, stuffing around on their skateboards. A couple of them looked up uneasily as a guard strolled past.

"OK," said Dad, "so, where does that get us?"

"Not far," sighed Jordan. "Our main problem is still the cameras. We've got no chance of even getting close to the medical centre unless we can find a way to knock that network offline again."

"Is there anyone back in town who might be able to help us?" Dad asked. "How about that security officer? The one who let you into the Weirs" house."

"The guards wouldn't have a clue about how to disable the new network," said Mr Weir, shaking his head. "No-one does, except Shackleton's top brass."

"What about Dr Montag, then?" asked Mrs Weir. "He's pretty high-ranking, isn't he? And he tried to help us before."

"He tried to help *himself* before," I corrected bitterly. "Who do you think's been making all these people "disappear" in the first place?"

It felt so weird, doing this stuff by committee. So far from me, Jordan and Peter making snap decisions in the back of an English class.

"Look, the cameras are going to be a problem," said Mr Weir. He stood up and started pacing the room again. "But they're not going to be our biggest problem. Not for long. That's what I was trying to say before. This new recruitment program – it's the biggest media push the Co-operative has ever done in Phoenix."

"They're planning something big," Jordan agreed.

"There were rumours flying around the office, last time I was in there," said Mr Weir. "A major announcement that was meant to be coming up. I never found out what it was, but..."

"But what?" said Mr Burke.

Mr Weir shrugged. "The mood in town is changing. You've seen it, right? Those blood screenings rubbed a lot of people the wrong way. Throw in this run of disappearances, and – and yeah, the *Herald* is always right there with a neat little explanation, but—"

"But there's no neat little explanation for the Co-operative abducting a six-year-old," said Mr Burke.

"Things are getting out of hand up there," said Mr Weir. "I think people are starting to ask questions."

"About time," Jordan muttered.

"Maybe," I said. "But that's not what Shackleton will be thinking."

I looked back down at the computer screen – people chatting in line at the bakery. Were they still talking about work and sport and whatever? Or were they actually noticing what was going on around them for a change?

I glanced over and saw Kara watching me. She was sitting completely still, with a look on her face like she was seriously disturbed by something but trying not to show it.

"We'd better get on with it, then," said Jordan. "The longer we wait—"

"Whoa, guys." I jumped up. "How long has that been up there?"

The camera angle on the laptop had just shifted again, pointing straight at the front doors of the

Shackleton Building. A big white banner was stretched over the entrance. The Co-operative's red phoenix logo, and two lines of huge letters:

COMPULSORY TOWN MEETING
8.30 p.m. Wednesday 8 July.

"Well," said Mr Weir, coming around to look. "I'd say that probably qualifies as "something big"."

Whatever Shackleton was planning, it looked like we wouldn't have to wait long to find out what it was.

Chapter 28

"Back in a sec," I said, reaching past Jordan to pick up her bowl from the table. I stood up, yawning, and carried the remains of our dinner across the hall to the kitchen.

Once the meeting had wrapped up, Jordan and I had stayed in the surveillance room for the rest of the day, scouring the town for anything else that might help us. But despite what Mr Weir had said about the changing mood up there, life seemed to be going along pretty much the same as usual.

Unless you counted Mum's office. That had been abandoned all day.

I crept past Dad, asleep on his bunk, and found Mr Weir on his way out of the kitchen, carrying a bowl of two-minute noodles and a mug of cloudy water. "Just going down to give Pete his dinner," whispered Mr Weir. "Anything you want me to tell him?"

I shook my head and he disappeared down the hall. We still hadn't been back to see him since his outburst on Saturday night.

I took our bowls to the sink and rinsed them clean. We were eating better than when we were hiding out next door to Mum, but not by much. Kara and Soren's pantry was stocked up with enough food to last *them* for months. But with the sudden population explosion down here, it wouldn't be long until supplies ran low.

I stuck the bowls on the drying rack and rested against the kitchen bench for a moment, staring out at the bedroom. Dad had crashed in there a couple of hours ago – but only after making several loud comments about giving Jordan and me some privacy.

I headed back out into the hall and almost ran straight into Kara, who'd come charging out of one of the bedrooms. Something scratched against my arm as she brushed past. She stuffed it into her pocket, but not before I had a chance to see what it was.

A battered old envelope, sealed with black wax.

Which answered our question about whether or not Kara was still communicating with Mike, Cat and Tank.

"Hey!" I said, grabbing her.

Kara wheeled around. She was crying. "Don't," she said fiercely. "This doesn't concern you."

Are you kidding me?

"Hey, Jordan!" I called. She didn't answer. "Jordan, I think you're going to want to—"

A huge, choking gasp from next door drowned out the rest of my sentence. Kara wrenched herself free and ran off down the hall.

I bolted into the surveillance room, just in time to see Jordan go crashing to the ground on all fours. She retched violently, rolling on to her side. I knelt next to her and shoved a hand under her head to keep her from smashing into the concrete.

"Jordan! Jordan, no, come on. Come on, just—" I held on to her arm with my other hand, doubting if she could even hear me. "Just – *breathe*, OK? Don't—"

I gasped, toppling forward, hand slipping from Jordan's arm. Slipping *through* Jordan's arm. Her head crashed through my other hand, smacking to the floor.

"Hey – no, come on, don't do this to me."

But she was already gone. The shaking stopped, and she rolled away from me, groaning.

Jordan sat up, eyes flying around the room. And instinctively I followed her gaze, like I expected to see what she was looking at.

Whatever she was seeing, it wasn't pretty. Jordan got to her feet, still trying to take in the whole room at once. She rushed to the door, unsteady, like Mr Weir when he first got his legs back, dodging invisible obstacles on the ground.

She stuck her head out into the empty hallway. But clearly it wasn't empty for her, because she recoiled straight away, stumbling back in my direction.

"All right, Jordan," I said. "You can come back now." But my hands just closed on air again.

Jordan stopped at the doorway across the room, peering in at the lab. I walked up behind her. "Jordan, seriously, time to— *No! No, what are you—?*"

Jordan was...

I could *see through her.*

She was fading. Like a ghost. Like her body was slipping away to wherever her mind was.

I clawed out in front of me, hands falling through her. "Jordan!"

She turned around, eyes wide.

"Jordan?" I said, reaching out again. "Hey! Hey, listen—"

Jordan's dad came bursting through the door at the far end of the lab, just in time to see my arms pass straight through Jordan's waist again. His mouth dropped open.

"What's going on?" Mr Burke demanded. "What did you—?"

"JORDAN!" I yelled.

She stumbled back, looking at me. Her mouth opened, shouting a reply, but no sound came out. *Luke!*

"Jordan!"

She reached for me, and I grabbed at her arms, still not able to touch her. Jordan's dad pushed forward, but he couldn't feel her any more than I could. And she was getting fainter.

"Jordan!" I looked straight through her eyes, the lab getting clearer and clearer on the other side. "Focus. You can hear me, right? Just keep listening to me."

She stared back, terrified, still mouthing words soundlessly. *Luke, I'm not—*

She broke off, spinning to look over her shoulder.

"Come on, Jordan, please, you have to—" My hands passed through her again.

I can't!

"Jordan, no— *No!* You are not disappearing on me!"

Luke, I can't—

"– reach!"

And suddenly her fingernails were clawing into me, digging into my forearms. She was coming back, getting solid again.

Mr Burke reached in to grab her. His arms passed straight through and almost smacked me in the head.

I held tight to Jordan's arms. "That's it, just – just look at me, OK? Just keep—"

Jordan jerked forward, head crashing into mine. I stumbled, but caught her before she fell. She clamped down even tighter on my arms and started shaking again.

"Jordan!" Mr Burke shouted.

"No, it's OK!" I said, bringing her to the ground, hoping I was telling him the truth. "She's OK now. She's going to be—"

Jordan let out a series of loud, gagging coughs, tears rolling down her face. She gave one last shudder, and then sat up, wiping her mouth. "Thank you," she said, still breathless, dragging me down into a hug. "Thanks. I thought…"

Mr Burke knelt down next to us, waiting until she

finally released me. "What was that?" he asked, still completely spooked. "Do either of you know what just happened?"

Jordan looked at her dad, then back at me. "I don't—"

There was a shout from back up the other end of the surveillance room, and Mr Weir came running in. He hesitated, seeing us all down on the floor. "You guys all right?"

"Hard to say." I got to my feet, pulling Jordan up after me. "What's going on?"

Mr Weir turned to look at her. "Peter wants to talk to you."

"Yeah," said Jordan wearily. He'd been asking for her every time someone brought him a meal. "I know. I *will* go and see him. I just need to find the right time."

"All right, sure, but—" Mr Weir's expression shifted. "I reckon that time might be now."

"Why?" asked Jordan. "What did he say?"

"He thinks he can – OK, look, I don't want to get anyone's hopes up, but if he can actually do what he's saying, then—"

"Then *what?*" I said.

"Then we're going to want to let him out as soon

as we can."

"Let him out?" said Jordan's dad. "Why would we—?"

"Because," said Mr Weir, "he says he's found a way to shut down the security cameras."

Chapter 29

"Jordan, wait!" called Mr Burke, chasing us down the corridor. "I don't want you rushing in there without—"

"I'll be careful," said Jordan. "Trust me."

We came to Peter's door. His parents had been down yesterday to help put his room back together and, apart from a few scattered book pages and the chipped furniture, everything was looking normal again.

"Can you two wait back here?" I whispered to Mr Burke and Mr Weir. "Probably better if we don't all rush in at once."

Neither of them looked too happy with this suggestion, but they hung back a few steps behind us.

Jordan peered through the gap in the door. I crept up and looked over her shoulder.

Peter was sitting cross-legged on the bed, attention fixed on the laptop we'd given him, back when he first moved in. Completely calm. No trace of the furniture-throwing psychopath from a couple of nights ago.

He glanced at the door and his eyes lit up. "Jordan!"

Jordan stood back, bumping into me. She muttered a quick apology and started lifting the bars away from the door.

"Stop!" barked a voice from further down the corridor. "Move away from there!"

Kara, coming back from her mail run. Peter's dad moved to head her off.

"Don't be absurd," said Kara, trying to get past him. "You can't possibly—"

Mr Burke silenced her with a look.

As soon as Jordan pulled back the last barricade, Peter shoved the door open, almost wiping her out. "Jordan!" he groaned, arms snaking around her. "Jordan, I am *so sorry*."

"Don't worry about it." She patted him on the

back a couple of times, then pulled herself out. "Your dad told us—"

"Right!" said Peter, grabbing Jordan's hand and pulling her into his room, like the rest of us weren't even there. "Come on, I'll show you!"

He sat on the edge of the bed, pulling her down next to him and dragging the computer to his lap. I walked in after them, but didn't sit down.

"OK, so, last weekend," said Peter, minimising whatever he'd been working on, "when you guys were heading up to meet my mum and dad, I was watching my house to see if—"

"He's lying," said Kara from the doorway. "That computer doesn't have access to the feeds. Soren disabled all network privileges before we ... even..."

She trailed off as Peter brought up a surveillance image of his house.

"So anyway," he continued, taking one hand off the keyboard to give Kara the finger, "when the cameras got shut down, at first I figured someone must've gone into the security centre and physically screwed around with the system, right? Like Reeve did, back when—"

He faltered for just a second.

Officer Reeve's death wasn't the first or the last

we'd seen since all of this started, but it was still the one that messed with us the most. The one that felt the most like our fault.

"But, yeah, I did some digging," Peter went on, "and that's actually not what happened. Montag launched the attack remotely. And I guess he was in too much of a hurry to cover his tracks, because I got a pretty good look at how he did it. And I've been working on it, and – Jordan, I reckon I can make it happen again."

Jordan stood up. "You're serious? You actually think you can do this?"

"Yes," said Peter, like his life was hanging on it. "I mean, maybe not for as long. They'll be more ready for it this time, obviously. But, you know, it's not like you guys have given me much else to do down here but work on this."

Jordan sighed. "Peter…"

"How long?" asked Mr Burke, pushing into the room. "How long can you turn them off for?"

"If you let me out to the surveillance room," said Peter, attention still on Jordan as though she was the one who'd asked the question, "and if the workarounds I've come up with actually do what they're supposed to do…" He bit his lip. "A minute. Maybe two."

Mr Burke's face fell.

Brilliant, I thought. *What are we supposed to get done in—?*

I caught Jordan's eye.

Uh-oh.

"Perfect," she grinned. "That's perfect. Plenty of time."

Tuesday 7 July
37 days

I dragged the last shirt up from the water and twisted it around my hands, wringing it out. A dirty brown stream ran back into the tub at my feet.

My plans of finding a secret laundry down here had turned out to be wishful thinking.

I shook the shirt out again and handed it to Jordan. She stretched up, draping it over the rope we'd strung across the living room.

"Where were you?" I asked, finally giving up waiting for Jordan to raise it.

She wiped her hands on her jeans. "Huh?"

"Last night," I said. "When you were, you know … gone. What did you see?"

"I was—" Jordan ducked under the makeshift

clothesline, and I could see the anxiety on her face. "It was the future again. I mean, I assume it was, because—" She cut herself short, shaking her head. "The whole place was turned upside-down. Furniture everywhere, computers all smashed..."

"Peter?" I said, checking the door to make sure we were still alone. "Did he—?"

"No," said Jordan. "No, that's what I thought, but then I went to the hall, and there were – Luke, there were *guards* down here. And one of them was – I looked out there, and this chair came smashing down the hall, and – I think it was *him*. I think the guard made it move. With his brain or whatever. Like Peter."

I tensed, like they were coming in right now. "They found us?"

"Well, they found *here* at least. I didn't actually see any of us, so maybe we'll all be out by then. I don't know, but –" Jordan looked right at me, like she was getting to the part she really wanted to talk about. "– there's something else. Right before you pulled me back, I heard someone shouting behind me, and I turned around, and – it was the guard who threw the chair. I think he *saw* me."

There was a thump on the door, and Kara walked in.

"What do you want?" asked Jordan, the vulnerable look vanishing from her face before she'd even turned around.

And since when do you knock? I thought.

"It's seven-thirty," said Kara. "They're all waiting for you."

"Give us a minute," I said.

And, surprisingly, she didn't argue. She waited there a moment longer, then skulked back to the surveillance room.

"What do you mean he *saw* you?" I asked, as soon as she was gone. "How is that even possible?"

"Possible?" said Jordan. "Luke, I've been having visions of the future for like a month now. I think we can assume that all bets are off at this point."

"Yeah, but—"

"Come on," said Jordan, ducking back under the clothesline. "We'd better get in there."

"Wait," I said.

Jordan turned back. I looked at her for a second, not exactly sure why I'd stopped her.

"This is going to work," I said. "We're going to find Georgia and your mum."

She gazed back at me with the sort of scary intensity she always saved for right before we did something life-threatening. "Yeah. We are."

I kind of wanted to kiss her again, but I figured now was probably not the time.

Jordan grabbed my hand. "C'mon. Meeting time."

We headed for the surveillance room.

"How did this happen?" I sighed as we walked.

"What?" said Jordan.

"When did we start going to meetings?"

I could hear Peter getting stuck into Soren before we were even through the door. "Would you get that bloody thing out of my face? If I was going to kick your arse again, I would have done it already."

"Sounds like we're off to a good start," I muttered, heading inside.

Kara and Soren were sitting either side of Peter, auto-injector pens at the ready. Hard to say whether they were making him less or more likely to lash out.

Dad, Mr Burke, and Peter's parents were sitting around the table too. I sat down at one of the two free chairs, feeling like the chairman of the board of some corporation.

"Sorry we're late," said Jordan, taking the seat next to mine.

Dad winked and gave me a secretive little thumbs-up. I tried not to look at him.

"All right," Jordan went on, apparently not noticing, "so, like we told you, we think we've come up with a way to get into the medical centre and rescue Georgia and my mum. It's a *little* bit sketchy, but I guess if we just lay it all out for you guys, then – then you can tell us what you think."

"A little bit sketchy" was kind of an understatement. But we'd both figured that the meeting in town was the best opportunity we were going to get to pull this off.

"Shackleton's meeting starts at eight-thirty tomorrow night," I said. "We're thinking we'll leave here at about eight-fifteen. That'll give us time to get around to the south end of town, before—"

"Hold on," said Mr Burke, leaning across the table. It creaked under him. "I think we need to just step back for a minute. Jordan, I don't want you going up there again."

"Dad, come on—"

"No, Jordan. You could get *killed*. What kind of father would I be if I let you put yourself in danger like that?"

"Right, because I've been completely safe down here," said Jordan.

Peter flinched.

"It's not about that!" she said. "This isn't – you wouldn't even *be* here without me putting myself in danger!"

"Jordan, just tell us what we need to do," said Mr Burke. "Please. Explain your plan to us, and we'll go up there and—"

"No!" said Jordan. "Dad, you're not cutting me out of this!"

Mr Burke shook his head. "I'm sorry, Jordan. This isn't your decision."

I expected Jordan to come straight back with another argument. But she just stared down at the table, red rising in her cheeks.

Silence stretched out across the room. Now what?

My dad straightened in his seat. "You're right," he said, eyes locking on Mr Burke. "Jordan's your daughter. If you want her to sit this one out, then that's what she should do, but—"

Dad wavered for a second, suddenly emotional. "Listen," he said, "I *love* my kid. If anything happened to him, I'd – I would lose it. But these guys have already been in this for months now. No-one knows Phoenix better than they do. This is their fight too. And, as far as I'm concerned, it will be for as long as they want to keep fighting it. Because the bottom line is, as much as I want to keep my boy safe –" His voice shook again. "– I *can't*. There is no safe option here. Not for any of us. But if we pull these guys out, all we're doing is hurting whatever chance we have of putting any of this right again."

I didn't know whether to cry or run around the table and hug him.

Mr Burke put his head in his hands, watching Jordan with almost the same expression he'd had last night. Like she was slipping away, and there was nothing he could do about it.

"Dad, please," said Jordan. "I know you're just trying to keep me safe, but…" She trailed off, her hand reaching for mine under the table.

Mr Burke rubbed his face with his hands and sat back up. "All right," he said. "Let's hear your plan."

It took Jordan a second to realize what he'd just said. Then her face lit up and launched straight back into it. "OK," she said, releasing my hand. "So, yeah, we'll get to the south end of town by quarter to nine. Banksia Avenue, down past the park. Scout out the street, make sure everything's clear, then sit tight and wait for Peter to knock out the cameras."

"Right," said Peter, taking over, looking happier than I'd seen him in weeks. "At quarter to, I'll launch the attack on the network. Should only take a couple of minutes, but wait till you see the lights go out on the cameras. As soon as that happens, start running to the back door of the medical centre."

"Which we still don't have a way to open," I reminded him. "Mr Weir, have you got any ideas?"

"You're not picking that lock," he said. "Not in two minutes, anyway. It's going to have to be brute force, but I don't know what could—"

"How about this?" said Jordan's dad, snatching Soren's pickaxe up off the floor.

Jordan beamed at him.

Mr Weir smirked. "Yep. That should do it."

"Won't there be people in there?" asked Peter's mum. "I know this meeting is supposed to be compulsory, but that can't include hospital staff, surely?"

"It's pretty quiet in there after dark," I said, thinking back to the night I'd spent recovering from Crazy Bill's beating. "A doctor and a couple of nurses. With any luck, we won't even see them."

Then again, it was the *with any luck* parts where these plans of ours usually fell apart.

"Besides," Jordan went on, "we're assuming the people they've taken are actually being held *underneath* the medical centre, otherwise someone would've found them out by now."

Then to Kara, she said, "Where is it?"

Kara reached under the table and pulled out Jordan's black Phoenix High backpack. The one they'd taken the morning we arrived. Jordan dumped the contents of the bag on the floor. Then she turned it inside-out and felt under the lining until she pulled out a rectangle of plastic. A Shackleton Co-operative key card.

"Told you I still had it," she grinned at me.

Mr Weir's eyes widened. "Where did you *get* that?"

"Long story," said Jordan, flipping the card over in her fingers. "Anyway, that's pretty much it. Knock out security, then two minutes, tops, to get inside, and then – well, we'll see what happens when we get in there."

"That's it?" said Peter's mum. "That's your plan?"

"What's wrong with it?" said Jordan.

"*See what happens?*" said Mrs Weir. "I'm sorry, but – shouldn't there be a bit more to it than that?"

"Nope," said Peter heavily, "that's pretty much how we do things."

"There's not much more we *can* do," I said. "The medical centre is the one place in town that's never

269

had any security cameras in it. Whatever's going on in there, they obviously want to make sure *no-one* finds out about it."

Peter's mum frowned. "If that's meant to reassure me, it was a step in the wrong direction."

I staggered up the hall, half-asleep, feeling along the wall for the bathroom door. It was late. Or early. Night, anyway.

I found the handle, stumbled inside, and flicked the switch on the other side of the doorway, rubbing my eyes against the sudden, blinding light. Into the first cubicle. I stared down at the bowl, trying to wake up the part of my brain that knew how to aim.

My mind drifted back to the meeting. At least four of us would be making the trip up to the surface tomorrow night, or tonight, or whenever it was. Mr and Mrs Weir were still making up their minds, but if they came too, it would be everyone except Kara, Soren and Peter.

Jordan and I weren't exactly thrilled about that combination of people staying behind, but, since Peter had to be down here to deal with the cameras, we couldn't really think of a better solution.

I finished what I was doing and walked back out

without pressing the button. Now that there were so many of us using the water supply down here, Kara had brought in this gross rule about not flushing anything that didn't have solids in it.

I washed my hands and slumped back out into the hall. I was awake now. Awake enough that it would probably take me ages to get back to sleep.

Awake enough to hear the low voices coming from further up the hallway.

I glanced along the hall and saw a thin strip of light shining out from under Kara and Soren's bedroom door. I crept up until I was close enough to make out the words.

"You've made that much perfectly obvious," Kara muttered. "But regardless of whether you *like* them, the fact remains that we're stuck with them, presumably until—"

"*If* they make it back from the medical centre tomorrow," said Soren.

"Don't be ridiculous," said Kara impatiently. "We'll be seeing Luke again, at the very least."

I shivered. The way she'd said it, it was like she knew something.

Soren must have said something that was too soft for me to hear, because Kara snapped, "Of course

I don't *want* to believe it! My wishes are beside the point, and have been since before you were born."

"But he *said* it," Soren protested. "He was the one who told you—"

"I was *there*, Soren. I know what he said. And we were right to be cautious. But whatever the truth of the situation, they are plainly yet to discover it. The most important thing now is to ensure that we are in a position to find out when they do."

"What about Tobias?" said Soren. "We still don't even know who he is."

"That's precisely the point," said Kara. "Honestly, Soren, after everything we've learnt – do you really still believe that this Tobias we're looking for is a *who?*"

Chapter 30

"We have to at least *try* to ask her," Jordan whispered as we crept up on Phoenix from the south. "If Kara's still giving orders to Mike and the others, we need to know about it."

"You really think you're going to get anything out of her?" I asked.

"My dad might."

I stared up at the stars glinting down through branches of the trees. Whatever else tonight was about to throw at us, I couldn't complain about having sky above my head again.

"What else can she want from them?" Jordan

273

asked. "She's got Peter. And now she's got us too. Wasn't that the point of all this?"

"Jordan, seriously, when have we ever come *close* to knowing the point of all this?"

I heard our dads whispering behind us and felt suddenly self-conscious. It was so weird to have our parents tagging along. After so long with just Jordan and me, six people felt like an army.

At the first sign of streetlights, Jordan stopped walking and turned around to shush everyone. "All right. When we get there, find something to hide behind and *keep still.*"

She directed the last two words at Mr Weir, who grinned and saluted. It was the first time he'd been outside since he got his legs back, and I swear he would have cartwheeled all the way if there hadn't been too many trees in the way. Mrs Weir rolled her eyes at him.

Earlier that day, I'd heard Mr Weir arguing with her, trying to convince her to stay behind with Peter, but in the end both of them had come with us.

We moved in behind a little cluster of bushes, and I squinted up at the nearest camera pole. I was pretty sure I could still see the lights glinting out from under the little dome.

Jordan pulled her binoculars from her backpack. "Nope. Not yet."

I checked the time on Dad's watch.

8.42 p.m.

"Look," said Mrs Weir, somewhere off to my left.

Mr Ketterley, Shackleton's residential liaison, had just walked out of a house across the street, flanked by two security guards. He trotted up the front path, scratching his mutton chops, and then ducked across to the house next door.

"I thought he lived up behind the Shackleton Building," said Mr Burke.

"He does," Jordan murmured, handing me the binoculars.

I pointed them at Ketterley, watching as he stepped up on to the verandah of the next house. He knocked on the door, waited, and then pulled out a key and let himself in. The two guards filed in after him. A minute later, they re-emerged, moving on to house number three.

"They must be combing the whole town," I said, feeling my throat tighten. "Making sure no-one's skipping the meeting."

"Guess Shackleton wasn't kidding about *compulsory*," said Jordan grimly.

I passed back the binoculars and she returned her attention to the security cameras.

8.45 p.m. Any minute now. I pushed up from the ground, ready to run.

It was eerily quiet. I mean, sure, it was night, but even at this hour, there were usually a few late-night joggers or people coming back from dinner. It was like the whole town had been deserted.

Ketterley moved along to the next house. And the next. 8.51 p.m.

"Something's wrong," I whispered, low enough for only Jordan to hear. "Do you think Peter—?"

"Shh," said Jordan, eyes still fixed on the cameras, waiting for the light to blink off. "Give him time."

He'd be trying. I knew that much. If there was one thing we could count on from Peter, it was throwing himself into whatever he thought was going to make Jordan happy.

I still didn't know how to feel about that. Peter had been chasing Jordan since before I'd even arrived in Phoenix. And now, after everything that had been happening…

I don't know. Somehow, it felt like we were using him. 8.53 p.m.

We shouldn't have left Peter alone with Kara and

Soren. A few days ago, they were trying to kill each other, and now our whole plan rested on—

Another thought resurfaced, something I'd been trying to push aside since Monday night.

"What about your vision?" I said. "The security guards down at the Complex. What if that's tonight? What if we're not supposed to—?"

"*Not supposed to?* I thought you didn't believe in—" Jordan sprang to her feet. "*RUN! Run, run, run!*"

I shot after her.

Mr Burke exploded out of the bushes behind me, pickaxe clutched in both hands. The others were right behind us. Adrenalin pumped through me. Now the town seemed anything but quiet. It was all pounding footsteps and ragged breathing and blood thumping in my ears.

Ketterley and his men must've been inside one of the houses, because I couldn't see them anywhere. How much time had passed already? Thirty seconds? More than that?

Peter's mum was right alongside me, jaw clenched. I'd been worried she might not be able to keep up, but I guess you don't last very long as a kindergarten teacher if you don't know how to run.

I heard the *shink-shink-shink* of sprinklers as the

park came into view. We bolted across the grass, straight into a wall of cold mist. In front of us, Jordan and her dad veered around the abandoned skate ramp, cutting across in the direction of the medical centre.

The mall stretched out to our left now, strangely dark, restaurants all closed up early for the meeting.

"This place is – incredible," panted Dad, eyes sweeping around as he ran.

Yeah, I thought, *that's one word for it.*

We burst out of the park, out from the cover of the mall, and pelted across the main road out of town. For a split second, we had a clear view of the town centre, Shackleton Building punching up into the sky, security guards out front, waving those orange traffic-control lightsaber things to get the last few stragglers inside.

And then we were back out of sight, hidden in the shadows of the medical centre. Jordan led the way across to the door. We crowded in around it, right under the gaze of another security camera. Still offline. What had it been now – ninety seconds?

"OK, get back," whispered Jordan's dad, bringing the pickaxe up level with his shoulder.

I stepped away, scanning the street again, and my stomach plummeted as he sent the pickaxe slamming into the door.

Our school principal, Ms Pryor, was coming out of a house, about four blocks away, tailed by another pair of guards. Going door to door, just like Ketterley.

There was a creaking noise as Mr Burke dislodged the pickaxe.

I looked down the street again. Pryor had stopped in the front yard of the next house. She was silhouetted in the porch light and I couldn't see which way she was facing, but her body language told me she was definitely not happy about *something*.

"Jordan…"

"I see her!" she said. "But what are we supposed to do—?"

Another explosive crack and the deadlock came flying off the door. My eyes shot back to Pryor. She was gone.

There was a thump behind me as Mr Burke threw his weight at the door.

I swept the binoculars out over the empty street, then back across to—

"Luke!" Dad grabbed my arm, pulling the binoculars away from my face. The door was wide open, and Jordan and her dad were already racing inside.

I checked the security camera. Lights still off.

Dad gave my arm another yank, and we ran in after the others.

Chapter 31

"Did you see where she went?" I asked, rushing over to Jordan.

"Pryor?" said Jordan, as Mr and Mrs Weir ran in behind us. "Into that house, right?"

"Did you *see* that, or are you just—?"

"Out of the way, Luke," grunted Mr Burke, heaving a bookcase over and flipping it on its side to block the door. It wouldn't hold Pryor off for long, but it was something.

I looked around the room. The lights were on, which was kind of disconcerting, but we were alone, for the moment at least.

At first, I thought we were in some kind of store-room. There were glass cabinets full of medical supplies, and a bunch of file storage boxes piled up on shelves along the wall. But there were a couple of beds too, and they looked like they'd been recently occupied.

"They probably kept them in here for a while," said Jordan, running a hand over one of the beds. "Sedated them or something before they brought them through the hospital."

Mr Burke snatched up his pickaxe again. "Let's get going."

I pulled the door open a crack and peered out at the hallway. All clear.

I stepped through, head spinning a bit at the sudden wave of hospital smell. After a week down in that decaying old bunker, I'd almost forgotten how unnaturally *clean* everything was up here.

I tried to get my bearings as the others came out behind me, but I'd never been in this part of the building before.

"Which way?" I asked Jordan.

She wavered for just a second, then strode out to our left, where a corridor lined with hospital rooms branched off toward the front entrance.

The quiet was starting to get to me now. We passed door after door, all locked shut. Blinds closed over every window. Every room still and dark.

"This isn't right," breathed Mrs Weir behind me.

"This is a *big* facility for a town this size," said Mr Weir. "It would take something major for them to ever need all of these rooms."

I bit my tongue. *Like the end of the world, maybe?*

We rounded another corner, and suddenly we were right out in the open. We'd made it to the reception area at the front of the hospital, opposite the big glass entrance doors that looked out on the town centre.

Right across the street from the Shackleton Building. Jordan walked straight out.

I dropped to the floor at the end of the corridor. *"Jord—!"*

But then my brain registered the darkness. Everything was switched off out here. I rose back up, breathed a nervous sigh, and followed her across to look out the doors.

The guards with the lightsabers were now patrolling around the fountain. They wouldn't be able to see us, though. Not from across the street.

We were safe. *But if we'd walked out here with the lights on...*

"You realize we could've died just then," I said.

"We could've died lots of times," said Jordan, walk-ing away. "C'mon."

We crossed the reception, into the east wing of the medical centre. A few corridors later, we passed the room where I'd spent the night, all those weeks ago, after Jordan and I had been attacked by Crazy Bill. I pictured myself lying in that bed, getting questioned by Calvin and Pryor. Like we knew *anything* back then.

"What are they doing sending Pryor out there, anyway?" I asked. "Not exactly in her job description to be on patrol with security. Aren't they worried about blowing her cover?"

"I don't know," said Jordan. "I'm starting to wonder how much longer that's even going to matter." She froze, holding up an arm to stop the rest of us. There was light shining out from a room, a few doors up.

Jordan tiptoed forward, signalling the rest of us to stay where we were.

I crept up behind her anyway.

There was a narrow pane of glass above the door handle. On the other side, I saw a row of beds, all crammed together, each one occupied by a sleeping person in a hospital gown.

Jordan pushed closer and I leant in behind her.

"Is it them?" I breathed, through a sudden rush of nerves. "Can you see—?"

But then I spotted the mangled body of a security officer. The new recruit that Peter had thrown into the side of his house.

These weren't our guys. They were actual patients, everyone who was too sick or injured to make it to the meeting. They must have put them all together in the one room.

Jordan reeled away from the window, head smacking into my chin.

A face stared back from the other side of the glass.

It was a nurse. She threw the door open, clearly terrified, but standing her ground. "Get back! Get away from here!"

"Sonja?" said Mrs Weir, stepping forward.

The nurse stared down the corridor, mouth falling open. "Jessica! What is this? Where have you *been?*"

"That would be a bit complicated to explain right now," said Mrs Weir, glancing into the room behind her. "Are you the only one here?"

"Yes, everyone else is at the—" The nurse jolted in shock. "Wait a minute. *Brian?*" She gaped at Mr

Weir's feet as he came over to join us.

"Will they survive without you for a bit?" he asked, nodding through the door.

"What?" said the nurse, fixated on his functioning legs. "Yes. Yes, they're fine. I'm just here as a precaution."

"Good." Mr Weir's hand slipped to his pocket. "Really sorry about this, Sonja." He whipped out an auto-injector and stabbed it into her thigh. The nurse gasped, stumbling back against the wall.

"Brian!" said Mrs Weir, scandalised. She reached out, taking the nurse's arms. "It's all right. It's all right. It's only a sedative…"

I cringed at the look of horror on the nurse's face.

Peter's dad ducked into the room for a second, returning with a pillow. "Here, put this under her."

The nurse slumped down to the ground, out of Mrs Weir's grip. Mr Weir stooped, apologising again, and slipped the pillow under her head.

"No, wait," I said, "we shouldn't leave her out here. Someone might see her."

"Right," said Mr Weir, still hunched over her. "OK Sonja, I'm just going to put you through here with the others."

"No…" she groaned, but she was almost completely

gone by now.

Mr Weir hoisted her up and carried her inside.

"What did you do that for?" demanded Mrs Weir as he came back out, pulling the door shut behind him. "We could have just *talked* to her!"

"Yeah, we could have," said Mr Weir. "And what do you reckon Shackleton would've done to her when he found out she just let us go?"

The anger drained away from Mrs Weir's face. "All right. All right. Sorry."

"Almost there," said Jordan, walking again. "Come on."

She took us around one more bend and down a flight of stairs and there, at the end of another little corridor, was a heavy steel door, just like the one on Pryor's office.

Jordan pulled out her key card and waved it in front of the sensor. The door clunked open, on to a tiny, empty room with rough grey tiles on the floor.

"Wrong place?" said Dad.

But Jordan was already inside, searching around the walls. She spotted a power outlet over in the far corner and reached down to flick the switches.

Air blasted up from under her feet, and she jumped aside as a square of tiles started sinking down into the ground. It dropped down about five centimetres, then slid away to the side, smoother and gentler than the one above the Vattel Complex, revealing a staircase down through the floor.

Mr Burke stared. "You've been down here before?"

"We used the school entrance last time," said Jordan, starting down the steps, "but I guess they all open the same way."

"I see," said Mr Burke uncertainly. He ducked down after her.

I hesitated. We were assuming the cameras here in the tunnels had been replaced along with the others on the surface. This would not be a good time to find out we were wrong.

Bit late to back out now, I thought, following Mr Burke down. It was only about ten steps to the bottom; nowhere near as deep as the Vattel Complex.

I stopped again on the last step. Last time we'd gone into Shackleton's tunnels, it had been all blinding light and gleaming steel. Tonight, everything was dark.

Jordan pulled a torch from her backpack and flicked it on, sending light glinting off the silver walls. Three doors led off in different directions. Jordan pushed open the closest one and shone the torch down a long, narrow tunnel.

Mr Weir whispered something into his wife's ear as Jordan closed the door again.

"What's down there?" asked Dad.

"Shackleton Building," I said, trying to picture the town above my head. "The tunnels all join together at this bunker place. What's happened to the power, though? Last time—"

The room grew suddenly brighter and I jumped.

Jordan had just pushed open another door. Light streamed in from the other side. "Come on. This way."

"Wait," said Mr Weir. He glanced at Mrs Weir again, like he was looking for confirmation on something. She breathed in, steeling herself, and nodded. Mr Weir squeezed her hand. "We'll meet you guys back here."

"What?" said Jordan. "No. Where are you going?"

"Someone needs to find out what's going on in that meeting," said Mr Weir. "We're going to head up and see what Shackleton's got to say for himself."

"You can't!" I said. "You think you can just walk in there after—?"

"We'll go through here," said Mr Weir, opening the door to the tunnel again. "Duck up in the lift. Trust me, mate. I was here when they *built* this place.

I know a spot where we can listen in without getting seen."

He's been planning this all along, I realized. That was what they'd been arguing about before.

I looked at Jordan. She shrugged back. It wasn't like we could stop them if this was what they really wanted to do.

"Besides," Mr Weir grinned, reaching into his pocket and pulling out a whole handful of plastic auto-injector cartridges, "I've got enough tranquilisers here to take down King Kong. We'll be all right."

"OK," I said, head swirling with all the ways this could go horribly wrong. "So – what? Back here in half an hour?"

"Twenty minutes," said Jordan, chucking him the torch.

Mr Weir nodded. "Done. See you then."

They disappeared, and the rest of us pushed on through the door with the light shining through it.

We emerged into a short, wide hall, with a couple of rooms on either side and a big set of double doors at the far end, all locked from the outside. No more gleaming steel, though. Everything was hospital white again.

I tried the first door on the right. Inside there

was medical equipment everywhere. Scanners and monitors and vials of who knew what. And in the middle of it all, an unconscious figure, curled up on a hospital bed.

He was lying on his side, breathing deep and slow, hooked up to an IV unit on one side and a heart monitor on the other. Tiny white lines crisscrossed his skin, almost-invisible remnants of a nightmarish injury.

And even though a part of me recognized him straight away, I just stood there for the longest time, trying to understand what I was seeing. Because it was impossible, even by Phoenix standards.

Impossible.

"Office Reeve?"

Chapter 32

Jordan almost knocked me down in her rush to get to the bed, but I hardly even noticed. My brain was still too busy melting down at the insanity in front of me.

He's dead, I told myself.

"Officer Reeve!" Jordan shouted, heaving at his shoulders. "Officer Reeve, *wake up!*"

He's dead. You saw him die.

But Jordan kept shaking him, and he rolled on to his back, and groaned, and—

"Whoa!" he shouted, springing up. "Jordan! How – how did—? *What's going on?*"

"You're *alive*," I said, feeling like it was important

for someone to point this out.

"Yeah," said Reeve, pulling off the heart monitor stuff and swinging his legs over the edge of the bed. "What's happening? Is it over? Are we rescued?"

"No," said Jordan, "but you are."

Reeve grabbed her arms. "Lachlan. My kid. Is he OK?"

"He's fine," she said. "Your wife too. At least, they were the last time we saw them. But, Officer Reeve—"

"Call me Matthew," said Reeve. "I'm not Shackleton's bloody *officer* anymore."

"Um, OK," said Jordan.

That was going to take some getting used to.

"Everyone thinks you're dead!" I said. "The whole town – we went to your *funeral*."

"In that case," said Reeve, standing up, "you kids had better get me out of here, so we can go set the record straight."

Jordan couldn't stop smiling at him. She hesitated, holding herself back for maybe two seconds, then dived in, squeezing him around the middle.

"Oof! Right," coughed Reeve, patting her on the back. "Yep. OK – come on – better get going."

Jordan finally released him, and we raced out of the room.

There was a heavy thud from the other end of the hall as Mr Burke threw himself at the double doors. They rattled, but stayed closed. He stood back, taking aim with the pickaxe.

Dad had just walked out of the room opposite us. "Anyone in there?" asked Jordan.

"Empty," he said, shaking his head, and Jordan moved off to try another door. "Who's this?" Dad asked.

"Officer Reeve," I said, over a crunch of metal from Mr Burke's pickaxe.

"Matthew," said Reeve, extending a hand.

"Matthew," I corrected myself. "Dad, this is the guy who got us into the Shackleton Building so we could call you!"

"Hang on…" said Reeve. "It worked? But then—"

"Luke!" called Jordan from across the hall. "Get over here!"

"It's kind of complicated," I told him, running across to Jordan. "I'll explain later!"

Another huge crunch and a smash and the double doors gave way. Mr Burke shouldered them open and ran inside.

I found Jordon in another one of the side rooms, bent over another figure in a hospital bed. It was Jeremy. He was waking up slowly, groggier than

Reeve had been.

There was medical stuff in this room too, but it was different. A whole bunch of what I assumed were blood samples, all treated and dyed and lined up and labelled. And not just *little* samples, either. Some of these containers were the size of Coke cans.

No wonder he was out of it.

"Here," Jordan grunted. "Help me get him up."

I dashed over and grabbed his legs, and together we twisted Jeremy around into a sitting position. We sat down on either side of him and brought his arms up around our shoulders.

"Lauren…" he murmured, stroking me with his fingertips.

"Uh, no," I said. "Guess again."

We hoisted him up and started helping him out the door. I glanced down at one of the benches as we passed by, and had to close my eyes to control my gag reflex. A row of petri dishes, sealed off in a glass cabinet, all filled with this horrible red jelly stuff. And on top of each one, there was stuff *growing*.

Stuff that looked an awful lot like human skin.

"I missed you…" Jeremy mumbled, dragging my attention away again. His head rolled down on to my shoulder.

"Yeah," I said, hauling him out the door. "Great."

I looked down at my hand, already smudgy and discoloured in the places where I'd touched him. He was coming around, slowly figuring out how to use his legs again, but we were still supporting most of his weight. And clearly his *brain* wasn't fully—

There was a high-pitched squeal from around the corner. "JORDAN!"

A second later, Georgia came sprinting out of the open doorway at the end of the hall.

Jordan dumped Jeremy on top of me and ran.

Georgia leapt up, little hospital gown billowing, and crashed into Jordan's arms. The tears were streaming down Jordan's face before she'd even caught her.

"Georgia," she choked, squeezing her. "I'm sorry … I'm so sorry…"

Jordan's mum came hurrying out, more pregnant than ever, helped along by a red-eyed Mr Burke. Jordan ran over, still clutching on to Georgia.

"There are more inside!" called Mr Burke, pointing back into the room at the end of the hall.

"Right," said Reeve, running past him.

I lowered Jeremy down against the wall, glancing over my shoulder to figure out where Dad was.

"You're beautiful…" he said blearily, clinging to

me. "Beautiful. You ... you know that, right?"

"Seriously, Jeremy," I muttered, peeling him off, "you are *this close* to getting left behind."

Still no sign of Dad. I headed for the end of the hall, figuring he must be in there already.

The room behind the double doors was about four times as big as any of the others. There were about ten beds, but a few of them were empty. I guessed this was the main holding room or whatever. The place where they all got kept when they weren't being experimented on.

Around the room, people were starting to get up. Officer Reeve was helping a skinny bald guy to his feet. Amy, the crazy-fast girl, was already up and waking Mrs Lewis. Dad wasn't in there. I ducked out again, starting to worry.

"Luke!" A door opened to my right and Dad poked his head out. "You might want to look at this."

I walked over, breathing a bit more steadily. Dad held the door for me. It was the only room we hadn't been into yet, and—

No.

No way.

Almost the whole of the room was taken up by a big dome thing, all thick glass and heavy steel, with a low, round door at the front, just big enough to crawl through. The whole thing was humming, like there was something electrical going on inside.

Inside the dome, stretching up from a wide metal column in the middle of the floor, was a kind of sloped platform, tilted toward where I was standing. And lying on the platform, unconscious and shaved bald and naked except for a pair of dirty white underpants, was Crazy Bill.

I gaped up at the pale, scarred form, mounted there like some hideous giant butterfly, limbs stretched out in all directions, cuffed to the platform with what looked like magnets or something.

"You know this guy?" asked Dad.

"Yeah," I said, distractedly. "Kind of."

Between him and Reeve, I felt like I'd stumbled into Phoenix's freak-show version of *This Is Your Life*.

"You ready, Luke?" asked Jordan, walking over with Georgia on her hip. "I think we're… Oh."

"Gross!" said Georgia. "Why doesn't he have any clothes?"

I knelt down at the little round door, trying to figure out how to open it. I couldn't see a handle anywhere, but there was a little keypad on the right-hand side.

My hand hovered over the buttons. "We *do* want to let him out, right?"

"Of course we do," said Jordan, turning. "Dad! Over here!"

Mr Burke came over, pickaxe still clutched in one hand. He looked up at Bill and shook his head, like this place was just being ridiculous on purpose.

"Can you get it open?" Jordan asked.

Mr Burke swung the pickaxe out wide behind him and brought it down into the glass with all his strength.

Shink.

The pickaxe just glanced back off again. Not even a scratch. Mr Burke rolled his shoulders, wincing a bit. "Sorry. No good."

And now I was really regretting letting Peter's parents disappear. If this bubble thing was what I thought it was, it had been designed by Mr Weir, back before he'd known what the Co-operative was really up to.

Jordan came over for a closer look at the door. She crouched, studying the keypad. And then suddenly, she was putting Georgia down on the floor and rummaging through her backpack. She dragged a battered bit of paper up from the bottom of the bag.

It was covered in scribbled pen drawings, fragments of whatever she'd been able to remember from the bizarre overseer journal Mike had been keeping, back when we were still at school. She ran her eyes over the page for half a second, then reached down and punched four numbers into the keypad.

1 – 3 – 0 – 8

The humming sound inside the dome whirred to a stop. The cuffs around Bill's hands and feet fell away and clattered to the floor. Bill slid down from the platform and crumpled on top of them.

There was a hiss and the door popped open.

It took me a minute to recover. "*That* was in Mike's notebook?"

"Nope," said Jordan, stuffing the paper back into her bag. "It was on Montag's wrist, the night we broke into the Shackleton Building. I saw it when I flashed back there."

"When you *what?*" said Mr Burke.

"Can you get him out?" Jordan asked him. "We'll go round up everyone else."

Mr Burke's eyes narrowed as he clambered through the door. "When we get out of here, you and I are going to have a talk," he said, lifting Bill on to his shoulders.

"Still don't believe I'm seeing this stuff for a reason?" whispered Jordan, picking Georgia up again.

Everyone else seemed to be out in the hall by now, some looking more awake than others.

Reeve strode out from the end room. "Right. That's all of us."

"Just a sec," I said. "We've got one more coming."

"All right, listen," said Jordan, raising her voice to talk to the whole room. "I know you've all heard a bunch of stuff about how Luke and me are evil and dangerous and whatever, but hopefully your stay down here has convinced you who the *real* bad guys are in this place. So everybody just get ready to run, OK? We're getting you guys out of here."

Mumbles of agreement from around the room.

Finally, I thought. It was nice to have someone taking us at our word for a change.

I did a quick head count. Ten of them, counting Bill. I had a feeling Kara wasn't going to be too happy with us.

"Hey, Luke!" said Georgia, swinging out from Jordan's side. "That man looks like you!"

"Yeah, that's my dad," I said.

"Oh." She grinned up at Dad. "Hey, guess what! Your boy and my sister are in love."

Dad leant in closer to her, speaking in a stage whisper. *"I know!"*

Georgia collapsed into Jordan's shoulder, giggling hysterically. Then she straightened up and started hammering Jordan with her fists. *"See?* I *told* you!"

"Gentle, sweetheart," said Mrs Burke, grinning.

"Have they *kissed* yet?" Georgia asked Dad. But before he could answer, her fingers tightened on Jordan's arms. Georgia squinted, head tilting sideways. Then her eyes went wide, and she gasped. "You *have!*"

I didn't know whether to be embarrassed or freaked out. That had been more than just a lucky guess.

"Got him," said Mr Burke, lumbering out with Crazy Bill slumped across his shoulders.

"All right," I said. "Time to go." I remembered Jeremy, still half-asleep on the floor. "Can someone—?"

"Let go of me!" screamed a voice from back out at the entrance. "Rob – tell me where we're going!"

Mum?

The door smashed open.

Dr Montag came tearing out of the darkness, dragging Mum along with one hand, clutching a security officer's pistol in the other.

I backed up, smacking into Mr Burke. Behind me, the huddle of people in hospital gowns started to panic and break apart.

Officer Reeve burst forward, fists raised.

"Stop!" said Montag, levelling his weapon. "There isn't time!" His chest heaved. He was *scared*.

Montag's eyes darted from Officer Reeve to me. "We need to run," he panted. "All of us. *Now*."

Chapter 33

Suddenly, everyone was looking at Jordan and me.

I glanced at Jordan. At Mum. At the gun in Montag's hand, still trained on Officer Reeve.

"Please," Montag said. "You've got to—"

"All right," said Jordan, raising her voice again. "All right, yes, do what he says." She started running, leading the way back toward the entrance.

"No!" said Montag, waving his gun at the room with all the beds. "That way! Out the back!"

He ran at us, yanking Mum along behind him. People started to turn, either following the order or just trying to get away from Montag. Through the double doors at the end of the hall.

I saw Reeve over by the wall, bending to get Jeremy. "C'mon!" I said.

"Yeah," he grunted, hoisting Jeremy up on to his back. "Right behind you."

"She's half a minute back down the tunnel," said Montag, hauling Mum past me. "Maybe less."

"Who? Pryor?" I said, running again.

"Victoria." Montag shot me a dark look. "Dr Galton. On to me as soon as I cut the power."

"I thought you and Victoria *worked* together!" said Mum, completely lost.

"*You* cut the power?" I asked.

We charged into the room, and Montag started pushing through the crowd to a heavy-looking door off to our right.

"Out of the way! *Move!*" He dropped Mum's hand and pulled out his keys. "Who else would it have been?" he muttered. "I saw the cameras go down again, and—" He broke off, scrambling for the right key.

And you knew it was us, I thought. *You knew where we were going.* And now he was dragging security straight down on top of us.

Reeve raced into the room, carrying Jeremy on his

back, just as Montag shoved the key into the lock.

"Hurry, doc!" said Reeve, pushing the doors closed behind us. "We've got—"

BANG!

The doors blasted apart again. Reeve went flying backwards through the air. He sailed clear across the room, crashing down on to one of the beds along the back wall, Jeremy still clinging to his back. The smash as they landed was almost drowned out by gasps and screams and the scuffling of people ducking for cover.

A woman strode into the doorway. Before tonight, I'd only ever seen her on video, shutting the door on those two terrified construction workers, moments before Tabitha ate them alive.

Tall. Slim. Flawless features. Long, brown hair. She *should* have been beautiful. But there was something cruel and cold behind her eyes that cancelled out the rest of it.

Dr Galton looked disapprovingly at Montag. "Away from the door, Rob." As she spoke, a bed came rocketing across the room. It slammed into Montag like a speeding car, pounding him against the wall. I leapt back just in time to avoid going with him.

Mum ran over. *"Rob!"*

I whirled around. "No, don't—!"

Mum screamed, lifting off the ground mid-step. She shot sideways into the wall, colliding with the plaster at head height and dropping to the ground. Like a pigeon hitting a window.

"Emily, please," said Dr Galton impatiently. "You're the reason he's in this mess in the first place."

She was like Peter, I realized. She could make things move without touching them. But this was different. It wasn't just random, accidental outbursts. Dr Galton could *control* it.

"Please, don't hurt us!" called an older woman, cowering behind a pillow.

Georgia started whimpering. Jordan had her down behind a bed, one hand over her eyes, trying to shield her from what was happening.

Dr Galton stepped into the room. There was something strange about the way she moved, everything just a bit too fluid, a bit too precise. It made me think of mercury sliding around in a Petri dish.

Her gaze flitted back out to the hall. "What are you waiting for?"

Two security guards appeared behind her, looking almost as nervous as the rest of us.

It finally dawned on me that I was still standing

up, and I dropped to the ground, edging toward the closest bed.

Galton pointed out to her left, where two more beds rested against the wall. "Line them up along there," she told the guards, and the beds immediately tumbled out of the way to create space. "Everyone except for Luke and his mother. They're to be disposed of."

My blood ran cold. This was it.

"No!" groaned Montag, still pinned to the wall by the end of the bed. "Stand down. Do not—"

The bed reared back and smashed into the wall again, knocking the wind out of him.

The security guards stared at each other, apparently unsure whose orders they were meant to be following.

I peered out from my hiding place, searching for an escape route, eyes landing on the little side door that Montag had been trying to open. His key was still sitting in the lock.

Mr Burke stood up at the back of the room. He lowered Crazy Bill on to the nearest bed and started toward Dr Galton. "Please. There are children here."

"Abraham," said Dr Galton, "you're going to want to put that down."

Mr Burke's hand shot to the side, pickaxe flying

out of his grip. It spun through the air, narrowly missing Mrs Burke's head, and clanked to the ground next to the skinny bald guy I'd seen Officer Reeve helping before.

"Please," Mr Burke repeated, shaken but determined, taking another step forward. "We don't want any trouble."

Dr Galton looked like she might have laughed if she knew how. "Deal with him," she told the guards.

I glanced at the door again, weighing up my chances. Two seconds to jump up. A few more to get it open. Too long.

"I have given you an instruction, officers," Dr Galton hissed at the guards, who still hadn't moved.

"But – Dr Galton, the doctor said—"

She clenched her teeth. "Oh, honestly..."

The guards" hands jerked forward, pistols flying out from between their fingers. Without even looking back, Dr Galton threw out her arms and snatched the weapons out of the air.

A crazed shout from the back wall jolted my attention away. The skinny bald guy was up on his feet, hands wrapped around Mr Burke's pickaxe, charging at Dr Galton.

He got about three steps, then shot straight back

the way he'd come, like he'd been hit in the stomach with a wrecking ball. The pickaxe spun out of his hands and *whumped* into something.

A sickening cry ripped through the room. I turned my head, everything suddenly in slow motion.

Jordan was lying on the floor. Hands pressed to her side. Blood dribbling between her fingers, way beyond anything her body could fix.

There was a roar from across the room. Jordan's dad, charging at Dr Galton, face like a wild animal.

Galton shot him a disdainful look and the bed I was hiding under flipped into the air, wiping him out of her path.

Dr Galton was walking toward me before Mr Burke had even landed. She stretched out her arms again, levelling both the guards" weapons down in my direction. "I'd love to know how you did it," she said. "How you and your mother managed to bypass our genetic screening and get yourselves on to the candidate register."

I scrambled back from her. There was noise coming out of my mouth, but none of it was words.

I could hear Jordan moaning on the ground.

Dr Galton stopped, eyeing me curiously. "You don't know, do you? You don't know what you're doing here any more than I do."

And then I was rising slowly off the floor, drifting into the air like a soap bubble. I flailed around, trying to get free, but nothing I did made any difference. Galton lifted me up until we were eye to eye.

"Think of this as a mercy killing," she said, closing what was left of the gap between us. "It will be far less painful than the death you would have suffered if we'd left you for Tabitha to clean up."

I shivered as she brought the pistols down against my chest. Something blurred past me.

"NO!"

BLAMBLAM!

I collapsed to the floor again, crying out, eyes squeezing shut. My hands flew to my chest, feeling the place where the bullets had torn through my skin.

But—

But there was nothing there. No pain. Not pain like there should have been. And then I heard a gluggy coughing noise from somewhere above my head.

I opened my eyes. Dr Galton had turned aside at the last second, weapons pointed away to my right.

Montag stood opposite her. He coughed again, two bright red circles spreading out across the chest of his shirt. And then he threw himself at Dr Galton.

His hands wrapped around her neck and they fell to the ground, almost on top of me, both grunting and shouting. And there was blood everywhere, billowing out between them.

Dr Galton twisted around, fighting to get out from under him, but for some reason she wasn't doing her brain thing on him. She dropped the guns, gasping for air.

Someone was screaming. Mum. Suddenly right there on top of Montag, shaking him, telling him to get up.

"*Run,*" he spluttered, voice all wet.

Jordan moaned again from across the room.

I ran over to her, shoving the bed away. She'd dragged a sheet down from somewhere, and it was balled up against her side, bright red and sticky.

I bent down, arms hovering over her, helpless. "No, no, no, you're not—"

Mrs Burke was kneeling there, horrified, Georgia sobbing into her hair. I scanned the room, desperate. Mum was still at Montag's side, hysterical. Dad was behind her, trying to bring her away.

The guards bent down to help Dr Galton.

"No!" she croaked, still writhing under Montag. "He's dead already! Take your weapons! Stop them!"

Something flew past out of the corner of my eye, and I ducked. But it was nothing Dr Galton had done. It was Amy, the running girl, already over at the door, turning the key.

I reached down, sliding my arms under Jordan.

She groaned. "It hurts."

"Sorry," I breathed. "I'm sorry. I'm getting you out, OK?"

I looked up again. The door was open. Amy was already outside. "Go!" I said to Mrs Burke, who was still kneeling next to me. "Get out! I've got her!"

Jordan's mum nodded. She stood, taking Georgia with her. I hefted Jordan into the air, realising I was crying. Her mum and Georgia ran out the door.

I felt a hand on my shoulder. "Give her to me." It was Mr Burke.

"It's OK," I said, glancing past him at Crazy Bill, still unconscious on the ground. "I've—"

"*Give her to me!*"

"No – please – you have to take *him*. He's – he's too big. I can't—"

"Do it," Jordan murmured to her dad. "Take Bill. He's important."

Mr Burke looked down at Jordan, then back up at me. Then he reached over and hoisted Bill up on to his back again. He glared at me with a look as terrifying as anything else I'd seen tonight. "You *get her home.*"

I nodded, choking down a sob. "Yeah."

Dad had finally got Mum away from Montag, and was dragging her, screaming, through the door.

One of the guards had picked up his gun. He stepped in front of us. "Hey – stop—"

"MOVE!" boomed Mr Burke.

The guard shrank back, and we kept going, past the mess of arms and legs and blood that was Galton and Montag, out the door and into the darkness.

Chapter 34

We were in another corridor. Another dark, steel-walled tunnel under the town. There was a light shining off to my left, streaming down from the ceiling.

Officer Reeve was already up ahead, spotlighted, waiting for us. "This way!" he yelled. "Hurry!'

I ran toward him, my vision still blurred with tears. Jordan shuddered in my arms.

The light was coming from a room above our heads, at the top of another silver staircase. I passed Officer Reeve and staggered up, trying desperately to keep Jordan steady. Her dad came up after me, lugging Crazy Bill.

The room at the top was an office. Big desk, leather chair, lounges around a coffee table. I bumped into the desk, knocking over a little photo frame. It was a picture of Cathryn.

This must be her mum's office, I realized dimly. Louisa Hawking, another one of the Shackleton Co-operative heads. We were in the office complex where my mum worked. Where she *used* to work.

Mum was screaming hysterically, fighting against Dad, trying to get back down the stairs. Mrs Burke and Georgia were up here too. And Amy, jittering wildly, looking ready to jump out of her skin. Jeremy stood over in the corner, back on his feet, but holding the wall for support.

"They're coming!" called a voice from the bottom of the stairs. Mrs Lewis appeared in the tunnel, supporting the old lady who'd been hiding behind the pillow.

Jordan coughed weakly, then moaned, clutching her side. "Listen," I said, holding her against me. "*No dying,* OK?"

Reeve sprinted up the stairs with Jeremy. "Is that everyone?"

"No," panted Mrs Lewis, white-faced, "Simon and Daniel are still—"

BLAM!

Another bullet, somewhere down in the corridor. Georgia screamed.

"Close it!" shouted Reeve.

"But—"

"Quickly!"

And someone must have found the right power outlet, because the trapdoor started sliding shut.

Mr Burke dumped Crazy Bill on one of the lounges. He ran over and upended the big wooden desk, scattering its contents across the floor. Mrs Lewis grabbed on and helped him drag it across the entrance to the tunnel.

"Won't take them long to get that off," said Reeve, rushing to one of the unoccupied couches. "Here, give me a hand with this."

He and Mr Burke brought the couch over and dumped it on top of the upturned table.

"Better," said Reeve.

I heard a muffled hiss as the trapdoor started rolling back open, underneath the table.

Mum was still fighting, battering Dad with her fists. "Emily, *stop*," Dad said firmly. "He's gone. You need to focus."

Mr Burke hefted Bill back over his shoulder. He shot another distraught look at Jordan in my arms, then reached for the door. "This way," he said, and I remembered that he worked here too.

We followed Mr Burke out into a dark corridor lined with offices. Jordan coughed again. I could feel her blood soaking through my shirt, still warm, and somehow that reminded me of kissing her, and I felt a rush of guilt, sickened that *that* was what I was thinking of at a time like this.

"The back way," I said, two steps behind Mr Burke. "You're taking us out the back way, right?"

He looked over his shoulder at me. "I would be if there was one."

We bolted up to the end of the corridor, pushing through to a little foyer area at the front of the building. Amy shot over and pressed her nose to the sliding glass doors, staring out at the main street.

"Ms Pryor!" she gasped, in her weirdly accelerated voice. "And there are security people with her!"

Reeve ducked across and tried to force the doors open. No good. "She's coming out from the Shackleton Building," he reported, looking out across the street again. "Five guards with her."

"Move!" shouted Mr Burke, putting Bill on the ground. "Quickly, out of the way!"

Reeve and Amy jumped aside as Mr Burke went charging into the glass.

SMASH!

The doors didn't shatter right away, but they cracked pretty badly. He reared back and tried again.

SMASH!

This time he went straight through, momentum almost carrying him down the steps on the other side. He charged back in and swung Bill on to his shoulders.

"Come on!" he shouted, reaching a hand to help Mrs Burke and Georgia through. I saw blood glistening where the glass had cut into him.

"Which way?" asked Reeve.

"Right," I said, forcing myself to focus. "The airport road. And then out to the north. But – but we can't let the guards see."

I ducked through the smashed glass, freezing wind hitting me as soon as I got outside. I pulled Jordan closer as I ran down the steps.

The security guards were already closing in from the left, circling around the fountain. Pryor ran along behind them, barely keeping up.

I looked back as I reached the bottom of the steps. Dad was right behind me, dragging Mum along by the wrist. She'd finally given up fighting, and was now just trailing mutely after him.

"Stop!" Pryor ordered, as the guards formed a wide circle, moving in to cut us off. "All of you, stop where you are!"

Mrs Lewis froze at the top of the steps.

Jeremy threw his hands into the air. "All right! Don't shoot!"

"No!" I shouted. *"Keep going!"*

I spun around, looking for a way through. The eyes of a couple of the guards widened as they caught sight of Officer Reeve, but they held their positions in the circle.

"Down on the ground," Pryor demanded. "Hands on your heads."

Mr Burke stepped up behind me. "Here," he said, hefting Crazy Bill off his shoulders and dumping him on my dad. "Take him."

"No!" Jordan choked.

"Stop!" Pryor shouted again. "Do not move!"

Mr Burke stared down at me. "Get her home, Luke."

He ran at Pryor. She had about two seconds to

scream before Mr Burke crashed into her, tackling her into a garden bed. Two of the guards broke ranks, rushing in to help.

"*Daddy!*" Georgia cried.

Mr Burke roared, twisting around as the guards leapt on top of him. "RUN!"

I took off down the street, jolting Jordan with every step. My shirt stuck to my chest, wet with her blood. Mrs Burke made a horrible, grief-stricken sound and started after us.

Dad caught up, racing along beside me, cradling Bill awkwardly in his arms. Mum was with him, finally getting it together enough to run on her own. Reeve dragged Mrs Lewis along behind them, and—

And that was all.

Jeremy and the nameless old lady were both still back at the steps, cowering, facedown with their hands behind their heads. I couldn't see Amy anywhere.

There were still two guards coming after us. Officer Reeve started shouting something, and then the world ripped apart behind me as one of the guards pulled the trigger on their rifle. Somewhere behind me, Mrs Lewis let out a strangled cry. I kept going. Nothing I could do for her.

I could just make out the airport road up ahead,

stretching away into the darkness.

Mum wailed behind me. I looked back, terrified. But she was still there. Still running.

We reached the dirt path that led out to the airport. I kept going, straight along the road. Had to get out of sight of the cameras before we veered back toward the Vattel Complex. The lights of the town faded away behind us until I could barely see where I was going. I glanced back again. The security guards were gone. *Why?*

I slowed down, scanning the faces behind me, searching for an explanation.

Mum. Dad and Crazy Bill. Mrs Burke and Georgia. And Amy, somehow back with us.

"Where's Reeve?" I asked.

There was a shout from back along the path, and then footsteps. People rushing toward us.

"Into the bush!" I said, veering off to our left. "Hurry!"

We crashed down between the trees. Too loud.

"Wait," I hissed. "Stop! They'll hear us!"

Everyone stopped running. I crouched at the edge of the road, resting Jordan on my knees. Georgia started whimpering again.

"Shh," Mrs Burke urged her, barely controlling

her own sobs. "It's OK, sweetheart. It's OK."

Officer Reeve came jogging along the path. He slowed, breath ragged, hospital gown blowing around his knees. His hands were wrapped around one of the security officers" rifles. He looked back up the path. The guards were still coming.

One of them flicked on a torch. "Up there!"

"Reeve!" I hissed.

He turned, looking straight at me. "Thanks," he whispered. Then he veered away, charging into the bush on the other side of the path.

The guards shot straight past our hiding place, racing in after Reeve, following him away to the south. For a few seconds, I watched the light of their torches flicker away between the trees.

And then I got up and ran.

Chapter 35

For the next fifteen minutes I was just running and running, and trying not to slow down, and trying not to fall, and telling myself over and over again that Jordan was going to be OK. And then finally we were back underground, racing downstairs again, the trapdoor clunking shut above our heads.

Kara met us at the door. She'd come out from the surveillance room, and she had a look on her face like she'd just watched someone die.

She took one look at Jordan and said, "Quickly. This way."

Down the hall, into the lab. She yelled for Soren,

323

and he ran in from the next room.

"Put her down," said Kara.

I lowered Jordan on to the mattress while Kara crossed to the sink to wash her hands. Everyone else was flooding in now, rushing around the room.

Kara returned, drying her hands on a paper towel. "Is there anyone here with medical experience?"

No-one spoke up.

"Nobody?" Kara pressed. "All right. All of you, *out.*" She pointed through the door to the surveillance room.

Mrs Burke looked up. "I'm not—"

"OUT!"

I was still holding on to Jordan, one hand jammed between her back and her rucksack, the other wrapped around her legs. I hadn't moved since putting her down.

She looked up at me, eyes not quite focusing, and opened her mouth to say something. But before she could get the words out, she started coughing again. She closed her eyes, tears running down the sides of her face.

Someone grabbed me from behind. Dad. "Come on, Luke. Let them work."

Kara lifted up a pair of big, nasty-looking scissors.

"Hey!" I said, tightening my grip on Jordan.

"You are *in the way*, Luke," Kara snapped. She started cutting into Jordan's clothes, clearing the way to the wound.

Dad gave my arm another tug, and I let Jordan go. Soren practically shoved us out of the room.

"Where's Peter?" I asked.

Soren shut the door in my face.

I lurched across the surveillance room, barely conscious, fixated by the blood on my clothes, on my hands, all up my arms…

Dad put an arm around me, guiding me back out toward the hall. "Let's get you into the shower," he said. "Find you some clean clothes."

"No…" I pleaded. "I need to go back in there."

"They're looking after her," said Dad. "They'll make sure she's—"

Mum gasped and swore. She was leaning over one of the surveillance computers, looking close to passing out. I staggered over with Dad, my exhausted body finding some new store of adrenalin.

We were looking down on Phoenix's town hall, a big auditorium at the back end of the Shackleton Building. I'd been inside it once, when Peter's dad had taken us on a tour of the building, but I don't think it had actually been used before, at least since I got here.

Mr Shackleton was centre stage, gesturing animatedly out into the audience. Calvin and seven other security guards were spaced out along the podium, aiming their rifles out at the crowd.

Mrs Burke came up behind us, Georgia still wrapped up in her arms.

The camera angle shifted. The hall was packed. Almost every seat full. Some of the people were crying. Others cowering behind seats. Most just sat there, staring, terrified. More guards patrolled up and down the aisles, weapons ready to deal with any trouble-makers.

The view changed again.

"Look," said Dad, pointing at the screen.

There, crammed into the back row, looking as scared as everyone else, though not as surprised, were Peter's mum and dad. Caught. Apparently, Mr Weir was right. The mood in town *had* changed. And it had changed enough for the Co-operative to decide that the subtle approach wasn't going to cut it anymore.

The screen flashed back to Shackleton.

"I don't understand…" said Jordan's mum. "What is he *doing?*"

"He's changing the rules," I murmured.

Shackleton walked out from behind the podium,

arms wide, smiling like he wanted to give everyone in the audience a hug. And I didn't need to hear the words coming out of his mouth to realize that things in this place were about to start getting extremely ugly.

Chapter 36

"Tell me it's worth it," said Jordan, wincing a bit as she shifted her position on the bed. "All of this. All of the fighting. I just – tell me we're not just wasting our time."

At first, I didn't know how to answer. It always made me nervous when she started talking like this.

I wrapped my hand around hers, feeling the warmth of it.

She was OK. Again.

The wound was pretty deep, but the pickaxe had somehow avoided slicing into anything too crucial. The blood loss had been the biggest thing. Kara had given her some blood and stitched everything back together, but it would be a few days before Jordan was back on her feet. Hopefully there wouldn't be too much death-defying to do between now and then.

We were alone in the lab for the first time all day. Everyone else was in the living area, having a meeting to sort out how life was going to work down here, and where we were all going to sleep.

Everyone who'd made it down here, anyway. My parents, Mrs Burke, Georgia and Amy.

And Crazy Bill, although he probably wouldn't be contributing much to the meeting. He still hadn't come around yet. Kara wasn't sure if he ever would. Who knew what that machine had done to him?

"We're not wasting our time," I said finally, with more confidence than I felt. "I mean, I'm not saying we can beat them. I'm not saying we're going to win, but – look, you're the one who keeps telling me there's a reason for all this. And if that's true…"

I trailed off, losing track of who I was trying to convince. "If that's true, then it's true all the time, right? Not just when the reason is easy to see."

She looked at me like she didn't know if that was profound, or just stupid.

"And last night … we did what we went up there

to do," I said. "We got Georgia and your mum. They're safe."

"Yeah," said Jordan, "in exchange for my dad and—"

"Jordan, you can't—" I stopped again, choosing my words carefully. "Your dad knew what he was doing. He can handle himself. And, look, I don't want to sound heartless, but – I mean, better him up there than Georgia, right?"

Jordan's dad was OK. Alive anyway, which was as OK as he could be, under the circumstances. Mrs Burke had found him on the security cameras this morning. He was in the town hall, along with the Weirs and everybody else in town.

The whole place was quickly being transformed into a kind of concentration camp. The guards had started a food line out in the welcome centre. They were bringing a few people out at a time, shuffling them along at gunpoint, and then sending them back to their seats. I didn't know what they were going to do about showers or toilets.

"We need to go see Peter," said Jordan. Kara and Soren had sedated him as soon as he'd got the cameras down last night, and put him straight back in his room. "Has anyone told him about his mum and dad?"

I sighed. "Not yet. Although I guess he might've seen it for himself by now, if…"

"Yeah," said Jordan. "How's your mum?"

"She's – I don't know," I said. "Not good."

Montag was gone. Really gone. We'd seen Calvin heading out to the graveyard this morning with the body and a shovel. I'd wondered at the time why he hadn't got one of his hacks to do it.

Jordan nodded. "At least now she's—"

Someone knocked on the door. I looked up. "Yeah?"

The door clicked open and Kara walked in. "Can we have a word?" she asked.

Soren came in behind her, carrying the dusty old TV and VCR from the next room. He plugged them in on the bench nearest to us.

"There's something we need to show you," said Kara, locking the door behind her. She moved around to the other two entrances, locking them as well, then pulled up a chair across from me, on the opposite side of Jordan's bed.

I straightened in my seat, nervous.

Kara paused, lacing her fingers together. "It appears that our assessment of the situation up on the surface may have been somewhat … inaccurate."

Jordan laughed. It turned into a coughing fit and she rolled over, holding her side. *"Really?"* she said. "You think?" But she was less aggressive than she might've been if Kara hadn't patched her up the night before.

"You must understand," Kara said, "we have spent years labouring under the assumption that *you* were the ones responsible. We did this with the best of intentions, and with what we thought was the most reliable information. But in light of recent events…"

Jordan pulled a face. "What are you doing, Kara? Trying to apologize?"

"No," said Kara. "I am trying to explain."

"Wait a minute," I said. "Reliable information from *who?* Who told you it was us?"

Kara glanced over at Soren, who was hooking up the VCR to the TV. "I suppose it's best if I start at the beginning," she said. "Twenty-six years ago, my mother arrived in this area with a small group of graduate students to investigate a phenomenon that one of her colleagues had documented. The ground on which Phoenix now stands was curiously unstable. Shifting unexpectedly, almost as though whole pockets of earth were simply *disappearing*."

Kara paused, like she was expecting us to start asking questions, but I think we were both still wondering why she was telling us this.

"However," she said, moving on, "it quickly became clear that any explanation for this phenomenon was far beyond the scope of a small-scale geological survey. Over the next four years, my mother assembled a team of specialists, and sought funding to construct this research facility —" She spread her arms out at the room. "— at which point, I was brought aboard as team physician."

"And?" said Jordan. "What happened?"

Kara hesitated, apparently still working out how much she wanted to tell us. "We're still not entirely sure *what* they were. The team simply referred to them as *events*. They were always unstable," she said darkly, "sometimes dangerously so."

"Dangerous enough to destroy this place?" Jordan guessed.

"Most of the time, when the events happened, the damage was fairly insignificant," said Kara. "But the last event was different. It destroyed the entire research module, killing almost all of my mother's team."

"And your mother?" asked Jordan. "Did she—?"

"There was another consequence of the collapse,"

said Kara quickly, veering away from the question. "The whole area became saturated with a kind of..." She wavered, grasping for the right word.

"Fallout?" I suggested, piecing it together, remembering the word Shackleton's people had used.

I watched the surprise register on Kara's face. "Yes. We believe this – this *fallout* to be what fuelled the sudden appearance of the bushland above our heads, as well as—"

"Peter," said Jordan, cutting her off. "And Dr Galton, and Bill, and that guard I saw." She stopped short of adding herself to the list, but I could see she was thinking it.

"Quite possibly," said Kara. She took a couple of deep breaths. It looked like we'd finally got to the point of her story. She glanced at Soren, who pulled out an old black video tape, pushed it into the machine, and pressed play.

A grainy, black and white image flashed up on the screen. There was no sound. It looked like security footage of an empty laboratory, from a camera up on the ceiling. Footage from back when this place was still up and running.

"Hey," said Jordan slowly, "is that—?"

"The room Soren excavated last week," Kara

finished. "Yes. This footage was recorded just over twenty years ago. It may help to explain some of the antagonism we—"

Something was happening on the screen.

A sort of haze had appeared at the far end of the room, like leaking gas. At first it was pretty hard to see, but it quickly got brighter and more obvious, until it was more like steam or something. It was maybe two metres across, rippling and swirling and—

And then a person fell out of it. Dressed in a tracksuit, hood pulled up over his head. He just *appeared* through the haze, like it was a door.

The person backed into the room, stumbling a bit, then righted himself and turned around, taking every-thing in.

Jordan's fingers clenched around my arm. I stopped breathing. Felt my body go cold.

It was *me*.

The guy who'd fallen into the room on the screen. Me.

I watched myself look back into the haze, just in time for someone else to come charging out.

Peter. He ran at the me on the screen, angrier than I'd ever seen him. He was holding something.

"No!" gasped Jordan, sitting up in her bed.

Peter was holding a knife. And he swung back his arm, and he pounded the knife down into my chest.

Jordan shuddered, fingers digging into me again.

Peter dragged the knife back out, teeth bared, screaming. The other me swayed on the spot.

"What is this?" cried Jordan.

Peter slammed the knife down again. And again. My legs caved, and I hit the laboratory floor with the blade still hanging out of me.

Peter glanced back through the haze behind him. He crouched, dislodging the knife.

I watched the screen, sick and terrified and not understanding *at all*.

Peter stood, looking straight up at the camera. And then he ran back through the haze, disappearing from the room again.

The me on the screen rolled over, screaming. He pushed to his hands and knees, leaving behind—

Leaving behind the blood that still stained the floor, out in that room.

And he started crawling. Bleeding and bleeding. Determined. Dragging himself across the room and out of the shot.

"That's when I found you," said Kara, almost whispering. "I was twenty-seven. Pregnant with

Soren. You – you came up the corridor, as far as you could before you collapsed. You were *desperate* to tell me something, to deliver a message." She sighed deeply. "A message that, in hindsight, I may have misunderstood."

I tore my eyes away from the screen. Jordan had her head in her hands.

"What—" I stammered, the words only just coming to me. "What did I say?"

"You were … not entirely coherent," said Kara. "But you told me people were in danger, that everyone was going to die. And you gave me four names. The three of you, and – and *Tobias*. You told me I had to take Tobias to the release station. Do either of you know what that means?"

"I don't know what *any* of this means!" I said.

"Why didn't you just *ask* us?" croaked Jordan, looking up. "Why – why all of *this*?"

"Because we thought it was you!" said Kara, voice rising. "Luke, when I found you, the way you were speaking – it sounded as though you were saying that *you'd* done it, that you were the ones responsible for—"

"*How?*" I said. "How could we *ever*—?"

"Why not?" asked Kara. "If you could generate these events, to transport yourself back to us … How

337

was I to know what else you could do? Not to mention – watch. Watch the screen."

I looked back at the TV. The video was still playing. An empty room again. But that haze was even brighter now, swirling faster, more violently, light radiating out, filling the lab. For a second, the screen flashed white. And then the picture dissolved into static.

"That was the end of the Vattel Complex," said Kara. "The project was shut down, the facility was – ostensibly – concreted over, and the few survivors we could account for returned home, though not before being sworn to secrecy by the company that backed the research."

"But you stayed," said Jordan. "This whole time, you've—"

"Not the whole time," said Kara. "At first, we spent much of our time on the outside, gathering information. But, yes, eventually we settled here to await your arrival."

"Wait," I said, all of it running together in my head. "What – what happened to me? After I spoke to you..."

Kara shook her head. "You were dead less than a minute after I found you."

Dead.

You were dead.

I felt like I wasn't here, like all *this* was happening on a TV screen too.

"When?" I asked. "When is this meant to happen?"

"Soon," said Kara. "From what you told me, I assume that you appeared from sometime *before* the Shackleton Co-operative's countdown expired."

"Thirty-five days," whispered Jordan.

It was insane. Impossible. But, for once, there was no doubt in my mind that Kara was telling the truth. Sometime in the next five weeks, I was going to *be* that other me I'd just seen getting murdered on that video.

Which meant that even if we found this Tobias thing, whatever it was...

Even if we stopped Tabitha...

Even if we *won*...

I'd still be dead, twenty years before any of it even mattered.

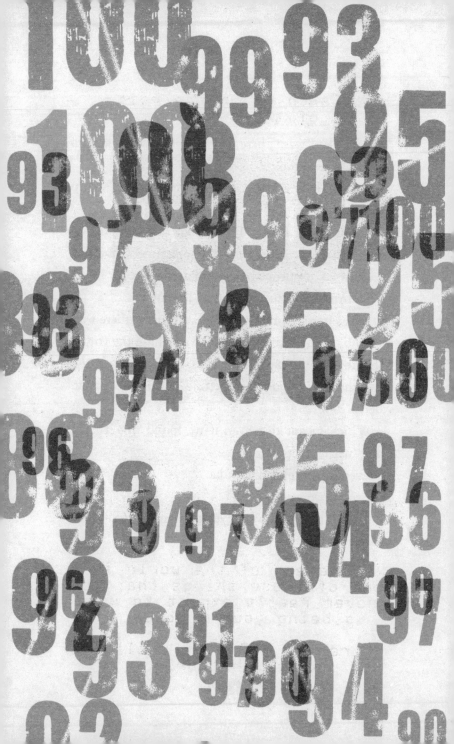

Catch up on the rest
of the series...

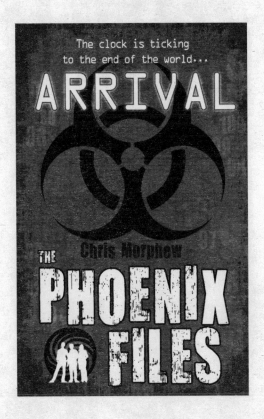

"The end of the world is
one of those things that you
never really expect to wind
up being your problem..."

There are 100 days until the
end of the world...

88 days until the end
of the world...

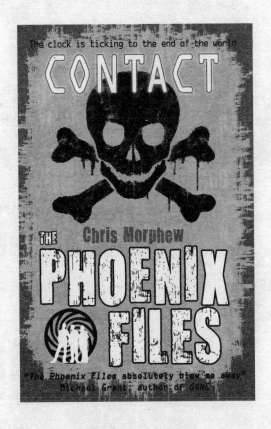

"One day off between suicide
missions. Was that really so
much to ask?"

63 days until the end
of the world...

"Phoenix was the one
place where people weren't
supposed to die..."

Look out for FALLOUT,
coming soon...